Sin City

Sin Club

RACHELLE CHASE

APHRODISIA
KENSINGTON BOOKS
http://www.kensingtonbooks.com

APHRODISIA are published by

Kensington Publishing Corp.
850 Third Avenue
New York, NY 10022

All Kensington Titles, Imprints, and Distributed Lines are available at special quantity discounts for bulk purchases for sales promotions, premiums, fund-raising, and educational or institutional use.

Special book excerpts or customized printings can also be created to fit specific needs. For details, write or phone the office of the Kensington special sales manager: Kensington Publishing Corp., 850 Third Avenue, New York, NY 10022, attn: Special Sales Department, Phone: 1-800-221-2647.

Aphrodisia and the A logo Reg. U.S. Pat & TM Off.

ISBN-13: 978-0-7582-1651-9
ISBN-10: 0-7582-1651-3

First Kensington Trade Paperback Printing: December 2007

10 9 8 7 6 5 4 3 2 1

Printed in the United States of America

Contents

Acknowledgments

To my family, as always, for without you I would truly be nothing. I love you.

Special thanks to: Hilary Sares, for letting me bring Sin Club to life . . . Leigh Michaels, for being my friend and colleague, as well as patiently listening to my zillionth "brilliant" idea . . . Alicia, who once again answered my last-minute desperate plea to critique this book . . . Calista Fox, for being my partner in crime at conferences, my sometime critique partner, and friend . . . Dan, for tirelessly upholding his role as my personal stalker . . . Mary B. Morrison, Lori Foster, and Sue Grimshaw for the awesome support . . . and, of course—most importantly—readers who read my books.

Prologue

Transcript of Interview with Dr. Tommy "Love" Jones on San Francisco's Number One Morning Television Show, *Wake-Up Bay Area*.

Wake-Up Bay Area theme song plays in the background. A red leather couch flanked by two brown suede chairs is situated in front of a floor-to-ceiling backdrop of the Golden Gate Bridge. Dr. Tommy "Love" Jones, wearing a black scoopneck T-shirt and khaki pants, sits on the couch, arms spread along the back, legs crossed, looking out at the audience with a smile.

Glass-topped coffee table, empty except for a red ceramic coffee cup, sits immediately in front of Dr. Love.

Wake-Up Bay Area host Lisa Mann, dressed in a powder blue suit, sits in the chair to the right, diagonal to the couch, with her legs crossed, coffee cup in hand, smiling faintly, her profile to the camera.

Music ends.

ANNOUNCER: Wake-up, Bay Area!

LISA: (*to audience*) Good morning, Bay Area. Today, we'll be talking with Dr. Tommy "Love" Jones, host of the popular radio talk show, *The Sin Club.*

(*turns to Dr. Love*) Welcome, Dr. Love.

DR. LOVE: (*smiles*) Thank you, Lisa.

LISA: *The Sin Club*—such an interesting name. I know our viewers are dying to know the answer to this question: How did *The Sin Club* get its start?

DR. LOVE: (*laughs*) By accident. When I took over the midnight show at KPSX several months ago, I kept the format open. Listeners could call in and talk about whatever was on their mind. Before long, I noticed a pattern. More than half of the folks seemed to be calling in with relationship problems. So I focused the show on relationship empowerment and called the show *The Sin Club.*

LISA: (*frowns*) But ... The Sin Club ... what does that have to do with relationships or empowerment?

DR. LOVE: (*leans forward, his expression serious*) Most people who called in were unhappy in their relationships but rather than doing anything about it, they settled—and complained. So I encouraged them to "sin."

What's the accepted definition of "to sin?"—to commit an offense. To these people who were settling and complaining, taking action to solve the relationship problem was offensive to them.

So my definition of "to sin" is to take action. To go after what you want. If you're not happy in your relationship, do something about it. If your partner is not treating you right, don't accept it. If your old methods of getting what you want are not working, try new ones. If you want that man or that woman, go after him or her. (*laughs*) Well, only if you're both single.

LISA: (*nods and sips coffee*) You make it sound so simple.

DR. LOVE: It is. Deep down inside, I believe people know what they want, know what they should do. They know when they should leave a relationship and they know when they should stay. Part of "sinning" is listening to that little voice, breaking out of your comfort zone, and taking action.

LISA: If it's so simple, why is your show so popular? (*leans forward, sets cup on the table, and grabs her notepad, reading notes*). I mean, in less than three months your show has gone nationwide.

Your midnight broadcast is replayed twice daily. (*looks up*) Why can't people heed your advice on their own?

DR. LOVE: (*shrugs*) Why do people with a drinking problem join Alcoholics Anonymous? Or people with a weight problem join Weight Watchers? For support. Whenever you're trying to break a habit, it helps to have encouragement. *The Sin Club* is a safe, anonymous environment for people to get the encouragement they need to make hard decisions—and to report back on their success and failures.

With 50 percent of all marriages ending in divorce and about half of those who remain married being in unhappy marriages—not to mention the single folks in bad relationships—unhappy relationships are a big part of American society. That's why *The Sin Club* is so popular.

LISA: Unfortunately, we're out of time. Is there any advice you'd like to leave our viewers with?

DR. LOVE: (*grins*). Yes. Go sin.

LISA: (*chuckles*). All right. Great advice.

Thank you for taking the time to chat with us today, Dr. Love.

DR. LOVE: Thank you, Lisa. It was a pleasure to be here.

LISA: *Wake-Up Bay Area* will be back after these messages from our sponsors.

Wake-Up Bay Area *theme song plays in the background. Dr. Love is leaning forward, forearms resting on his knees, listening to Lisa. Lisa is talking, gesturing with her hand. Dr. Love nods and laughs, then begins talking.*

Music ends.

Cut to commercial.

Jessie

A Sinful Striptease

1

"*Today* is the day to sin ..." Dr. Tommy "Love" Jones's voice seemed to whisper the words directly into Jessie Anderson's ear.

Jessie turned from the window and frowned at the stereo speaker from which Dr. Love spoke. "I'm *trying* to sin," she muttered.

"Take charge—" continued Dr. Love.

"I am."

"Be bold—"

"I am."

"Do something you've never done before—"

"I am!"

"—something that you've always wanted to do, but never thought you could do. Because you were too scared to go after it. Or scared you might actually get it—"

"I'm not scared I'll get it."

"—Or scared you might *not* get it."

"Yeah, well, I am a bit scared of that one."

"So be bold. Take charge. Do it. Go sin. It's all about you . . . Tonya M., you're on the air."

Jessie turned her attention back to the window. She parted the gauzy curtain, careful to keep her nakedness hidden. As she peeked outside, she idly listened to the radio show. As Tonya M. described her deep-seated desire to give up psychiatry and become a mortician—and how her career unhappiness was affecting her relationship—Jessie shook her head. Why did the grass always look greener? Here Tonya wanted to flee the living and work with the dead, while all Jessie wanted to do was inject some life, some excitement, some *sex* into a member of the walking dead: Martin.

And today—tonight—was her last chance to save their relationship.

Jessie reached over and switched the radio off. She turned on the CD player. Sade's "Ordinary Love" soothed her frazzled nerves as she gazed out the window, ignoring the beauty of the ocean below. Instead, her gaze sought the backyard of the vacant single-story house next door. She stared intently into the blackness, able to make out the dark shadow that was the gazebo, nothing more.

No flicker of red light.

Jessie dropped the curtain and began to pace, her quick strides causing the flames of twenty candles to flutter erratically as she passed.

Where was Martin? He should have arrived more than thirty minutes ago. She was sure her written instructions had been clear: *Be at the gazebo of the vacant house next door. Flash the light on your key chain at 9:00 P.M. sharp*. Though Martin was a genius with numbers, erotic rendezvous were not his forte. But surely even Martin couldn't screw that up?

Maybe his penlight had gone out.

Heart racing with anticipation, body thrumming with excitement, Jessie rushed back to the window. Was that the signal? She craned her neck. Yes, a definite red flicker. She took a deep breath.

Take charge.

Be bold.

Do it.

Go sin.

Summoning the sexy vixen sleeping within, Jessie smiled in the direction of the signal, and flung open the curtains.

Nick Ralston gazed out over the ocean, admiring the moonlight as it bounced off the waves. He loved the sound of the ocean, so peaceful, so different from his life. But that was about to change. Making a fresh start wasn't going to be easy, but he'd taken the first step by buying this house. His house. Well, technically it wasn't his yet, but it would be by next Friday. For added insurance, maybe the "For Sale" sign out front would mysteriously disappear when he left. He smiled at the image of the large sign hanging out of the passenger side of his Porsche Boxster.

Leaning against the gazebo, Nick lit a Marlboro Light. He exhaled the smoke before it could enter his lungs and withdrew the cigarette from his lips, staring at the glowing tip. With a wry smile, he flicked his wrist and sent the cigarette spiraling to the damp grass. He ground the toe of his shoe against it, extinguishing it forever. He sighed. No women, and now, no cigarettes. Which one would prove harder to swear off?

With one last glance at the ocean, he turned to walk down the path separating his house from his neighbor's, heading to his car. He'd only taken two steps when a movement in the second story window of the neighboring house caught his eye. He glanced up and stopped mid-stride.

A woman in a red, see-through number stood in the window, silhouetted against a backdrop of flickering candles. Nick watched her lean forward and open the window. Muted strains of drums, guitar, and piano drifted over to him, accompanied by a sultry feminine voice. It took him a moment to realize that the throaty lyrics were not recorded with the music, but rather, were coming from the woman herself.

As she straightened, the hot curves of her body were once again visible. The bouncing light shone through the thin material, perfectly outlining the small waist and flaring hips that merged into lush thighs. Thighs that parted and hips that began to gyrate suggestively as he watched.

"What the hell . . .?"

As if in answer to his question, the woman took a step backward into the room. Candlelight illuminated her face enough for Nick to see her lips curl into a seductive smile. He watched her long, slender arms rise above her head, her wrists and shoulders rotating in sync with her hips. Her fingertips slowly traveled down her body, brushing lightly over her breasts, over her stomach, down her thighs, then back up, this time caressing her inner thighs and taking the hem of her gown with them. His breath stuttered in his throat as her hands stopped at her pussy, her fingertips making vertical circles while her hips moved back and forth to meet them. A brief glimpse of dark hair was visible with each upward movement.

Nick's hand went to his crotch.

The urge to unzip his jeans and stroke himself in time to the woman's swaying hips surged through him. Instead, he moved his cock to a more comfortable position. He knew he should leave. But, he couldn't. Her hips mesmerized him, keeping him rooted to the spot. Unlike the erotic acts he'd been forced to endure at bachelor parties, this woman's routine seemed . . . personal. Her movements unpracticed, spontaneous, and aimed directly at him, at his satisfaction. He didn't know why or how she even knew he was here.

But, hell, did he really care?

Her fingers stopped their lazy circling, the clingy material dropping back into place around her thighs.

"No . . ." Nick's whisper of dismay escaped him of its own volition.

Ignoring his need, the woman buried her hands in her upswept hair. A quick shake and ebony curls cascaded over her shoulders. She threw her head back, drawing Nick's eyes to her throat, infusing him with the desire to trail his lips along her neck, down to her shoulders, to nibble at her collarbone before licking—

His visual fantasy ended abruptly as her head snapped forward and she crooned to the waning music. Her lips—coated in a shiny red that shimmered with each word she sang—plucked a chord tied directly to his cock. A smile spread slowly over her face, as if she knew exactly what was happening to Nick. Then she spun around and sashayed to a chair he hadn't even noticed was in the room. Her back to him, she shimmied in front of the chair, her hands grabbing her ass, squeezing and massaging, her fiery nails glistening with each grasp.

Nick licked his lips and reached in his back pocket for the emergency cigarette before remembering it lay mutilated in the grass.

He let his hand fall back to his side.

The music changed to something slower and the piano was replaced by electronic keyboards. As the moody notes of a saxophone cascaded over his eardrums, the woman's hands caressed their way up her back and slid the straps of her gown over her shoulders.

Nick held his breath, waiting, hoping, praying . . .

As if in slow motion, he watched the slinky material slide over her skin, hugging her hips for the briefest moment, before gliding to the floor.

His erection surged against his jeans as he stared at the most perfect ass he'd ever seen. No anorexic model here. This one would give Marilyn Monroe a run for her money. Before he could look his fill at her backside, she turned around and Nick's mouth dropped open.

She was holding a stuffed bear. Only this was no innocent bear from Saturday morning cartoons.

She trailed the bear's face over her body, giving the impression it was bestowing kisses, licking and laving its way across her breasts. She held its head against one breast and rubbed it slightly back and forth.

Nick groaned. An unbidden desire surfaced to feel her hands threaded through his hair, pressing his face against her plump tits, to let his tongue flick across her dusky nipples, to feel them harden in his mouth . . .

He watched her change the bear's position, dragging it across her abdomen, lower, lower . . .

His breath became ragged. "Oh, yeah . . . that's it," he breathed, as she brought the bear's face to the dark hair that hid what Nick desperately wanted to see, to explore.

Suddenly, she turned around, her back once again to him. The bear's lower body dangled obscenely between the "v" of her thighs as she threw her head back and rotated her hips.

Nick closed his eyes, blocking out the sight of her full derriere swaying back and forth. He inhaled deeply and concentrated on getting his pulse and hormones back under control. He had to get out of here.

Now.

He'd ignore her. He'd walk back to his car, not once looking up at that window. Yeah, that's what he'd do.

He opened his eyes and took his first step with determination. By the second step, he felt his eyes drawn back to the window. Okay, he'd take one last look while he was walking. Before he'd completed his third step, he stopped and gaped at the window.

The bear had disappeared and the woman stood gloriously naked. Her finger curled and uncurled, beckoning. She turned, smiling at him over her shoulder, then moved from sight.

Nick remained where he was, stunned. This woman—this stranger—had just invited him inside.

His first thought was to take her up on her offer, to run, not walk, right up to that second story bedroom. But the voice of reason intervened, reminding him of his promise:

No women.

Sandy, hooking him with her flirtatious ways, keeping him with her passion and adoration, and sinking him with her lies, had been the perfect catalyst for his vow. While he'd been walking around proud to be her man, she'd been making other men proud—teasing them, leading them on, and sleeping with them.

No. He had no time for women, no time to try and figure out who was telling the truth and who was lying. He was here to focus on work.

No women.

Silently repeating the promise like a mantra, Nick continued along the path and stalked to the front of the house, determined to ignore the images of his naked neighbor and what she might be doing in bed—without him. When he reached the driveway, he opened the car door and paused. He turned around and glanced back at the now-empty window.

His cock still throbbed. His pulse still raced. Curiosity and anger battled in his mind.

Why the fuck had this sexy stranger beckoned *him*?

15

2

Jessie picked up the silk scarf from the bed, looped it around her head, and tied it in the back. She adjusted the silky material so that the world was black, the dancing flames gone as if she'd blown them out. She lay on her back on the bed, resting her head against the pillow, and raised one leg, bending it at the knee.

Her body tingled. Every nerve ending under her skin had been awakened by her hands as they'd traced her hips, trailed over her abdomen, and cupped her breasts. Desire, anticipation, and a hint of embarrassment coursed through her veins—a tinge of embarrassment because she'd never been so bold, never acted so brazen, never felt so sexy.

She'd implemented Dr. Love's advice. She was sinning.

But Martin had never seen this side of her before—would he like it?

Jessie frowned. What man wouldn't like it? Countless men's magazines—and women's, for that matter—were devoted to ways of spicing up your sex life. And hers and Martin's had disappeared. If this didn't infuse a bit of excitement, it would be the sign she'd been looking for, final proof that there was no relationship left to salvage.

Your relationship was over months ago. Sex isn't going to save it.

Jessie shifted her hips, crushing the thought, and letting the softness of the comforter caress her ass.

The soft whisper of the front door opening caressed her eardrums.

Footsteps, muted by the runners covering the hardwood stairs, sent anticipation humming through her body. Maybe she'd been wrong about Martin. Maybe there was something left in their relationship.

Jessie cocked her head. She couldn't see through the blindfold, but the creak of the floor told her that Martin stood in the doorway.

"Hi," she purred.

Martin remained silent.

Her body flamed, excited by the thought of Martin speechless. She arched her back and rotated her hips slowly. "Do you like what you see?"

He inhaled sharply.

She slid her hands over her breasts, plucking a nipple. Darts of delicious prickles zoomed to her pussy. She moved her hands lower and cupped her mound.

Martin exhaled noisily.

Jessie lifted her hips. "Pussy got your tongue?"

She chuckled at her pun.

He didn't laugh. The only sound was the sigh of his uneven breathing.

He didn't move. Tension emanated from his body and spiraled through the air and stroked her body, empowering her, arousing her.

Jessie returned one hand to her chest, circling her breast.

"Did you like watching Teddy lick my nipples?" With her other hand, she rubbed a finger along her clit. "Did you like watching Teddy taste my pussy?"

Her hips rose, beckoning him closer.

The floor in the doorway creaked again as he obeyed. The whisper of fabric brushing together started—then abruptly stopped—at the side of the bed.

Jessie looked up at him with eyes unable to see, imagining his eyes roving her body, seeing flushed skin, her turgid nipples, and her wet pussy.

The bed dipped to the right with his weight.

"I want you to—"

Martin's fingertips silenced her as he traced her mouth and down her neck, to the swell of her breasts, following the path hers had made. The pads of his thumbs rubbed her nipples.

"Oh," she breathed, jutting her breasts forward into his palms. "I like that. It's been a long time since you've touched me, Martin."

The fingertips left her skin abruptly.

"Don't stop."

He remained unmoving.

"Martin?"

He remained silent.

Oh shit. Don't tell me he's chickening out. If he was, this was it—officially the last straw. Jessie frowned and sat up, her hands going to her blindfold. "Martin, what—"

"Shhhhh—" Martin whispered. His hands pressed against her shoulders, gently pushing.

Jessie sank back onto the soft downy bed.

Martin leaned forward. She inhaled the faint scent of cigarette smoke and spicy cologne she'd never known him to wear before. Maybe he'd bought it for this occasion.

She smiled. "You smell good. Did you—"

His mouth replaced his fingertips, interrupting her thoughts as he nibbled her neck. His tongue traced her collarbone and moved down, dipping in between the valley of her breasts, before turning inward and circling her areola.

Jessie moaned. "Oh, I like that."

She moved her hands to his shoulders.

His hands instantly circled her wrists, pulling them away, returning them to the side of the bed by her head.

She got the message—he wanted her to lie there and let him do whatever he wanted to do. The roughness of his hands gripping her wrists—so unlike their usual softness—sent a bolt of excitement swirling through her stomach. Her heart thrilled at the effort Martin was exerting to make this special. He was taking charge and playing along with her game.

It was more than she'd hoped for. Never would she have thought that he had it in him. Sex with him had always been so routine and predictable. But maybe she'd been too quick to judge. Maybe there was hope for their relationship. Maybe she hadn't done a good job of showing him what she wanted. Well, that was going to change. Starting—

Once again, Martin took her nipple in his mouth and sucked.

Jessie sucked in a mouthful of air.

Spears of heat spread through her breasts, building in her stomach, and spilling over into her pussy.

Jessie wriggled her hips and arched her back higher, wanting to feel more of him against her than his lips. She wanted to grab his head and press him closer. She wanted to wrap her legs around his chest and pull him against her. What she didn't want was for him to stop, so she didn't touch him.

Instead, her hands grabbed fistfuls of the comforter and her hips rocked against the bed. "I want more," she begged.

His lips moved to her other breast.

Her hips bucked. "I want you to li . . ." *lick me.*

She caught herself before she said the words. Martin wasn't into oral sex—giving or receiving. They'd had numerous arguments about that. Despite his new willingness to play along, she wasn't going to open that can of worms. Things were going too well. Her body was buzzing with sensation, her skin straining to touch his, her pussy reaching for his cock, her limbs aching to circle him.

"I want you to fuck me," she said instead.

A groan rumbled in Martin's chest.

A shiver rippled through her, excitement humming through her body by his response to her first use of the F word with him.

His mouth left her breast, trailing over her stomach, alternately blowing hot and cold air, causing her skin to quiver.

Fabric rustled and the bed dipped more to the side, as the cloth of his shirt—cotton?—brushed her thighs seconds before he positioned himself between her legs. His knees inched her legs open wider while his lips nibbled lower, kissing her naked flesh.

"Martin . . ." she whispered in amazement. Oh, my God. He was going to do it. "Oh, Martin . . ."

His hands slid under her ass, gripping each cheek.

His tongue darted between her lips, lapping her swollen clit.

His hair brushed against her inner thighs, caressing her with feather-like strokes as his tongue slid lower, entering her like a miniature cock.

The heat that had pooled in her stomach flooded her pussy, seeking the fire ignited by his lips, the flames stoked by his tongue.

Jessie thrust her hips forward, urging him deeper.

Martin answered her plea. His tongue rammed her pussy, his moustache slightly abrading her lips.

21

His hands massaged her ass, the calluses dotting his palm contributing to the roughness of his grip.

His head bobbed between her thighs, the silky strands of his hair caressing her flesh.

All of this caused the pressure inside Jessie to build and—

Jessie froze.

The orgasm—seconds away from exploding within her—evaporated.

Mustache.

Calluses.

Silky hair.

Seconds ago, the feel of these things caressing her skin had teased and aroused her. Now they repulsed her.

Martin did not have a mustache.

Martin's hands were smooth from working computer keys all day.

Martin's crew cut felt spiky—not silky—against her flesh.

Heart crashing against her ribs, Jessie jerked upright and scooted towards the head of the bed. She yanked off the blindfold.

Through the "v" of her legs, chocolate brown eyes framed by long, dark lashes, stared back at her.

Nutmeg brown hair fell across his forehead.

His full, kissable lips glistened in the candlelight—glistened with her juices.

Jessie screamed.

3

Nick's sluggish brain grappled with the fact that his tongue no longer delved into hot flesh—no longer tasted the spicy muskiness of hot pussy—and quivering thighs no longer clutched his head.

He blinked, trying to focus on the terror-filled brown eyes staring back at him.

The high-pitched scream that nearly split his head in half cleared the fogginess from his brain, providing instant clarity.

He stood and backed away from the bed, holding his hands up halfway in a gesture of surrender.

Still screaming, the woman dove for the side of the bed, rummaged around under it, and stood. She gripped a Louisville Slugger baseball bat, her stance resembling a batter at home plate awaiting the pitcher's throw.

The sight of the naked, five-foot-three-inch tall woman clutching a bat almost bigger than she was, itching to knock him out of the room, should have made him smile. Granted, it would be a wary smile, because adrenaline might give her the strength to break a few of his bones, even if she couldn't send his ass flying from the room.

Instead, as Nick took in the tangled black curls spilling over her shoulders, his hands itched to bury themselves in her hair, pull her head back, and kiss the succulent lips he'd wanted to plunder when he'd had her blindfolded beneath him. Her heaving chest made him crave holding a breast in each hand, squeezing and massaging, while watching her nipples grow hard—

Hard.

Just like his cock.

He gave an inward snort of disgust. Rather than smiling or indulging in lust, what the sight of the small, naked woman trembling in front of him should instill was the desire to reassure her, to calm her.

"I'll use this," she warned, shaking the bat.

"I know," he lied, trying to prevent his eyes from noticing that the end of the bat was close to her flat stomach, inches from the baby smooth flesh that he'd been tasting. A hint of the clit he'd been probing peeked through her still-swollen lips.

His cock lengthened painfully.

Nick, once again, shifted his stance in an attempt to get comfortable.

The woman also shifted her stance, placing one leg in front of the other, pressing them tightly together as if attempting to hide from his gaze.

Just like Pinocchio's nose, his cock grew. Though it felt like feet, not inches.

Shit. Focus, Ralston.

He raised his gaze, noticing her arms clutched together, as if she were trying to hold the bat and hide her breasts at the same time.

Focus.

24

Nick lifted his hands higher in the air. "Look. I'm going to turn my back and risk you splattering my brains on this wall . . ." He turned and faced the doorway, praying his hunch that she wouldn't use his head as a baseball was right. "Now, cover yourself . . ."

All he heard was her jagged breathing.

". . . and let me know when it's safe . . ."

Safe for who? You or her?

". . . to turn around."

After seconds of continued silence, the rustle of clothing greeted his ears.

"Turn around," she said.

He turned.

She'd donned a red robe. The silky material clung to her hips, tracing her thighs and her mons, as if molded to her body by a slight current of static electricity. Her breasts tented the front of the robe, the nipples forming spiky peaks.

Obviously, her robe had done nothing to make either of them feel safer: Her ruby-tipped fingernails still gripped the bat; his rock hard cock still strained against his jeans.

Nick suppressed a sigh.

The only good sign was that anger had extinguished the terror that'd filled her eyes previously. This was a good sign because it meant progress had been made. The line between anger and passion was much easier to cross than that between terror and passion.

And Nick wanted to see her brown eyes sparkle with passion.

No women, remember?

Yeah, he'd remembered all the way across the yard to her front door, and up the stairs. He'd planned to march into the room and ask her what the hell she was doing. But when he'd

25

stood in the doorway and stared at the luscious curves spread on the bed like a sinful buffet, he'd forgotten both his pledge and the plan.

"Who are you?"

"Nick Ralston." He smiled, hoping to put her at ease, then stuck out his arm, and took a step forward.

"Don't move." She waved the bat threateningly.

"Why don't you put the bat down?" He forced his voice lower, softer. "If I was here to hurt you, I could've done it a long time ago."

Her grip on the bat tightened. "What *are* you doing here?"

Good question, Ralston. "You invited me."

"I invited *Martin.*"

"Yeah, well, I didn't know that, did I?" *Well, not until later.* "Surely you don't think any man who saw your hot body gyrating naked in front of a window would be able to resist? . . ." Nick frowned. ". . . And just where is Martin?"

Color flooded her face. But based on her pursed lips, he guessed it was anger—not embarrassment—that had turned her cheeks rosy.

Her cheeks had been rosy minutes ago, too, when he'd been sampling her juices, but the pink hue sure as hell hadn't been due to anger or embarrassment.

Martin was obviously a fool. What man in his right mind would stand up such a hot, sexy, woman waiting for him?

A moronic asshole, that's who.

"Who's Martin?" the question slipped out, his tone sharper than he'd meant for it to be. And before he could stop them, a couple more words trickled out. "Your husband?"

Shit.

Prior to this moment, he hadn't considered the fact that she might be married. He made it a rule to never mess around with another man's—

"No, I'm—" Her mouth snapped shut and her chin jutted forward.

Nick smiled, relieved.

"But that's none of your business. The point is *you're* not Martin."

"No. I'm not Martin." Nick remembered her words when his fingertips had caressed her. "Unlike Martin, I touched you."

She gasped, drawing his eyes to her lips—lips that had been parted, just like they were now, when he'd been licking and kissing her other lips. Those lips had been parted, too. Partly by his tongue, as it'd slid from her pussy to her clit, but also because they'd been swollen.

Swollen with desire.

His cock swelled and he took a step forward.

"Don't." Her voice was shaky. Her grip loosened and the bat wavered.

He ignored her words, paying attention to the slight glaze in her eyes and the rapid rise of her chest, and took another step towards her. "Why's it been a long time since Martin's touched you?"

His slightest touch had sparked her body; she'd been on the verge of coming the second his lips—barely probing, hardly lathing—had caressed her hot flesh.

That knowledge had left him seconds from creaming his jeans—something he hadn't come close to doing since Honors English in junior high, when he'd fantasized about Ms. Jenkins giving him a blow job.

There was another possibility. "Is Martin impotent?"

"No!"

Nick took a final step until he was standing a couple feet in front of her, within batting distance. He wanted to lean down and kiss her, but the panic-mixed-with-lust expression on her face told him her response wouldn't be what he wanted. In fact, he might actually get clubbed by the bat, like she'd been promising. So instead, he reached out a hand and brushed his fingertips across her forehead and down her cheeks.

She inhaled sharply, drawing his eyes and his fingers to her mouth. He traced her upper lip. "When you asked, 'Do you like what you see?' my answer was ..." He traced her lower lip. "... and still is, yes."

He trailed his finger over her chin and down her neck, feeling her throat bob as she swallowed. "And when you asked, 'Did you like watching Teddy lick my nipples ...'"

He slid his fingers over the round swell of her breast and across her nipples.

She gasped.

"'... and taste my pussy?' my answer is yes."

He let his fingers follow the front of her robe, barely touching, past the sash, pausing at the bottom of her stomach. "I liked tasting your pussy. It was hot and spicy and sweet all rolled into one. And I want to taste it again."

He licked his lip, savoring the faint taste of her that lingered.

Her gaze dropped to his mouth, following the movement of his tongue. "Please. Leave."

Her whisper was strangled.

Yeah, Ralston. Leave. No women, remember?

Well, his plan was going to have to change. He'd stick to his pledge to give up cigarettes. How could any man—except Martin—be expected to hold out when presented with the luscious temptation in front of him? It'd be okay if he didn't give up *this* woman because this wasn't about a relationship.

She wouldn't get in the way of work.

If you say so, buddy.

His tone was determined. "When you realize Martin can't give you what you need, let me know."

He dropped his hand and stepped back. His cock was sending urgent messages to his brain—the command to take her in his arms, lead her back to the bed, and convince her to let him prove Martin's incompetence. He felt that she'd let him. The desire was rolling off her in waves, she was trembling with it, and he could smell her desire.

But the small twinge of guilt over the knowledge that he was encroaching on another man's territory—and taking advantage of her—pricked his conscience and forced him to keep walking. This had to be her decision, should she choose to get rid of Martin.

When she'd called you "Martin," why didn't you stop?

The sight of her blindfolded, gyrating her hips on the bed and touching her breasts, coupled with her words about that damn stuffed bear, had banished every thought from his head—except the desire to fuck her. And when he'd stroked her silky skin—softly with featherlight caresses—and she'd begged him not to stop, he'd wanted to hear her beg him again. And again. And again.

When she'd called him Martin, he'd paused, and tried to gather the strength to stop, but . . .

Well, at least he hadn't had sex with her.

You fucking licked her cunt. What's that considered?

Well, he was walking away now, making up for it.

You fucking licked her cunt. Little late to be walking away now, isn't it? Might as well turn around and finish things.

He really had been planning to stop.

But he hadn't—and wouldn't have, had she not stopped him.

*Turn around, man—she's yours **now**. What if she never dumps Martin?*

4

Jessie ran down the hall and stopped at the top of the stairs, all the while keeping her eyes on the broad-shouldered stranger. He walked down the steps as if he didn't have a care in the world, as if he knew he was safe from the bat she still held. In fact, it wouldn't surprise her if he started whistling.

She should knock him upside the head just to prove that she could do it.

But she couldn't do it, nor did she *want* to do it. Instead, she wanted to call out to him and ask him to stop, to come back. God, what was wrong with her? A stranger had walked into her house, dipped his head between her legs, and used his tongue in places and ways that Martin never had.

Was she feeling outraged?

No.

Scared?

No.

How about violated?

No.

Instead, she felt confused and aroused. Nervous and aroused. Ashamed and aroused.

Aroused, aroused, and aroused.

Something seemed wrong with that. Like there should be a case study with her name on it in *Psychology Today*.

She watched him reach for the doorknob and turn it.

When you realize Martin can't give you what you need, let me know.

Martin hadn't given her what she needed—physically or emotionally—in months. She knew that but thought she'd make one last-ditch effort to rekindle . . . something.

Yeah, well, she'd rekindled something, all right. Just not with Martin.

Nick opened the door.

She gripped the banister with her free hand.

When you realize Martin can't give you what you need, let me know.

She didn't even know how to contact him, so how was she supposed to let him know what she needed? She shook her head in disgust. It was *good* that she didn't know his number or address because there was no way she was going to contact a man who, for all she knew, could be a pervert.

Then why was disappointment seeping into her cells and flooding her body?

The click of the door closing spurred her to race down the stairs. Jessie locked the door, engaging the lock in the doorknob, as well as the deadbolt. Then she peeked through the window to make sure he was, indeed, leaving.

The meager moonlight illuminated the faint shadow of him on her stairs before the darkness swallowed him. She continued to stare into the blackness, straining for a sight of him, seconds before she heard the roar of a car engine in the driveway of the vacant house next door. Headlights snapped on, giving her a quick glimpse of a dark, sporty-looking car before he roared off into the night.

Jessie fell back against the door. Her body still hummed, but it wasn't with fear. Adrenaline pooled in her muscles, ready for action that had nothing to do with running.

Aroused, aroused, and aroused.

She closed her eyes. What was wrong with her?

5

Jessie opened her eyes, awakened by the flush of the toilet. She blinked several times and glanced around the room. When her eyes landed on the sputtering candles, she jerked upright.

Oh, God, had Nick come back? How could he have gotten back in her house? She'd watched him leave, saw him drive off, and had bolted the door.

The fear that she hadn't felt when she'd watched him leave flooded her system. Just as she scrambled out of bed, Martin came out of the bathroom in his white boxer shorts.

"Hi. Sorry I woke you," he said, yawning.

Jessie's heart stopped scrambling to break free of her chest. Taking in a deep, calming breath, she glanced at the clock. She'd been asleep for two hours—which meant it'd been two hours since she'd given a performance that should've had Martin rushing to her bed.

Only Martin hadn't seen it.

Surely you don't think any man who saw your hot body gyrating naked in front of a window would be able to resist?

Images of the brown-haired stranger with sexy eyes and a

lethal tongue, flickered through her mind. Of his mouth on her breasts, teasing her nipples, of his fingertips raking her thighs, making them quiver, of his tongue licking her flesh, bringing her to the cusp of orgasm.

Would Martin have done any of that, even if he had been there?

Her blood, once again, rushed through her veins. Anger and arousal swirled through her body. She pulled the silky robe closed and tightened the sash.

"What took you so long?" she asked, her tone deceptively calm.

"I had to work late." Martin's gaze flickered over her body, then he gestured towards the candles and frowned. "What are—"

"You had to work late."

Martin finally looked at her. His brows drew tighter together. "Yeah, you know about the audit next month. Smitherton wanted . . ."

Her blood crescendoed, drowning out the drone of his words. He'd foregone her stellar attempt to add some excitement to their nonexistent sex life for an audit? Not even bothering to call?

"Did you get my letter?" she asked.

"You mean the one the courier delivered?"

"I don't recall sending you another one. Did you read it?"

"I was going to but then Smitherton came in and . . ." he shrugged. ". . . well, you know how that is."

Yes, she did. Smitherton, Townsend, and Branson had been the cause of numerous late nights and cancelled weekend getaways.

Or so he'd said.

"I was going to open it, but I didn't think it was important."

"Martin, how often do I send letters to you at the office?"

He paused, studying her face. "Is this a trick question?"

"What?"

He sighed. "Okay. Never."

"Well, then, didn't it occur to you that it might be important?"

He glanced at the ceiling, as if seriously thinking about the question. Seconds later, his gaze returned to hers. "No."

Clueless, but honest. Gotta love that in a man. Or not.

Jessie tried a different approach. "Martin, can you remember when we last had sex?"

Martin's sigh was annoyed. "Oh, God, Jessie, not this again."

Jessie remained silent, waiting for his answer.

Martin raked his hand over his crew cut. "I think it was two months ago. That night you got me drunk."

"Exactly."

"Jessie, you know how hard Smitherton works me. I'm tired all the time and . . ." his tone was exasperated. ". . . who needs sex when we have . . . friendship."

"*I* need sex, Martin. And I'm not sure we have a friendship."

"What's that supposed to mean?"

"We don't talk—not about our day, not about our dreams, not about anything."

"That's not true. Why, just last week, we talked about . . ." Once again his eyes drifted to the ceiling. "Uh . . ."

"Exactly."

His gaze sharpened. "Jessie, this Smitherton partnership is crucial to me. I've worked hard for it. It's all I want. I don't have time for a . . ."

Jessie raised a brow. "Relationship?"

Martin remained silent.

"Exactly," Jessie said softly. She reached down and picked up his pants from a nearby chair, holding them out to him. "I think you'd better go now."

"I . . . I didn't quite mean it like that."

"Yes, you did. It's just not working, Martin. We both want different things."

Martin took his pants from her. "All right." He hurriedly got into his slacks and moved toward the door. In the doorway, he paused and turned to face her. "I'll come get the rest of my stuff next Sunday night, okay?"

"Sure."

"Jess . . . I'm sorry. I didn't mean—"

"It's okay, Martin. Good-bye."

He nodded his head, then turned away.

Jessie remained where she was until she heard the click of the lock on the front door. She realized belatedly that she should have asked him to leave his keys. Well, she'd get them when he came to pick up his few belongings.

She turned and walked around the room, blowing out each candle until only the dim light from the moon filtered through the drawn curtains to brighten the room. Once again, she walked to the window and parted the drapes. She peered out into the backyard, gazing in the direction of the gazebo—the gazebo where she'd thought Martin stood watching as she'd stripped and stroked her body, her skin tingling, her excitement growing as she imagined Martin's reaction, his erection, as he'd watched. And when she'd brushed Teddy against her body, imagining it was Martin . . .

She reached down and picked up Teddy, then leaned against the window frame.

"But it wasn't Martin, was it?" she asked.

Jessie stared into the bear's glassy brown eyes and moved his head side-to-side.

"And a mere stranger had made me feel better than Martin ever had, hadn't he?"

Her fingers forced Teddy's head up and down.

God, it'd felt so good—and Nick hadn't really touched her. No caresses, no kisses. He'd gone straight to her pussy without foreplay and she'd been hot. Hotter than she'd ever been. So hot that she'd had a hard time believing it was Martin.

At the time, little did she know she was right. Now, she was glad it wasn't Martin.

She hugged Teddy to her chest and turned her attention to the ocean.

Well, it was over with Martin. He was history.

She frowned. Wasn't this the point where the tears were supposed to course down her cheeks? The point where she was supposed to bang her head against the windowpane and shriek, *Oh, Martin!*

Jessie did a quick inventory of her feelings and her frown deepened.

Nothing.

She felt nothing, other than a sense of relief that she now had the whole closet to herself, that the top shelf of the medicine cabinet would once again contain her nail polish collection.

Absolutely nothing.

Except the lingering synapses of lust for a stranger. A stranger that she would never see again.

The thought made her wonder what he had been doing at the vacant house in the first place. She should've asked him. But, the roar of sexual feelings had deafened all rational thought.

Jessie sighed and turned towards the bed, taking off her robe as she went. She set Teddy down, slipped under the covers, and stared at the ceiling. She waited, again, for the loss of Martin to hit her, to suddenly wrap itself around her heart like a vise . . .

Instead, as she shifted her position in the bed, the feel of the silky sheets brushing her skin became the invisible fingers of a brown-eyed stranger, brushing her thighs and caressing her nipples. Jessie moaned softly and slid her hands under the covers, imagining that he—that *Nick*—was back in the bed with her.

She cupped her breasts, feeling his hands squeeze them.

She drew light circles against her flesh, feeling his tongue instead of her fingers.

"Suck my nipples," she whispered.

Her fingers, tugging on her nipples, were Nick's teeth.

The palm of her hands, rolling her nipples, became his tongue.

"Yes," she said, pressing her thighs together tightly, and thrusting her hips upward, then downward.

"Open your legs," Nick said.

Jessie uncrossed her ankles and spread her legs. She continued rolling the palm of her hands against her nipples.

His tongue continued licking her nipple.

Her hips continued fucking the air.

He stopped.

"No . . ."

"What do you want?" Nick whispered.

She slid her palms down her body, over her stomach, and down her hips.

He slid his hands down her body.

She ran her fingers along her thighs.

Nick stroked the sensitive skin of her inner thighs with the pad of his finger, before moving inward, lightly caressing her naked lips.

She bucked her hips.

"What do you want?" He breathed the words in her ear, now on top of her, with his fingers between their bodies. He slipped a finger between her needy lips and stroked.

Jessie arched her back, sucking in jerky breaths. "Yessss . . ."

Her fingers strummed her clit.

He rubbed her clit faster and harder. "What do you want?"

She spread her legs wider and ground her hips faster. "I want you . . . to . . . fuck me."

The F word, something she never said to a lover, caused her heart to skitter in her chest and her finger to dip inside her pussy, moving in and out and around and around.

Nick thrust into her hard and fast.

Jessie gasped at the shock of his entry. The heat searing her, spreading over every inch of her flesh, was no longer caused by her fingers.

His cock ignited her nerve endings and sparked her flesh.

Sensation was building . . . building . . . building . . .

"Please . . . Oh, I want it. Need it. Now."

Her finger flew over her clit.

His cock slammed into her.

Her hips jerked up and down, meeting him, forcing him to go faster.

"Shit," he said as he drove into her, seconds before his cock pulsed inside her pussy and his body quaked.

Spasms slammed through her body and waves of heat collided inside her. Her fingers slowed, then stopped.

"Thank you, Nick," she said when the last quiver had died. As she drifted off to sleep, her heart felt as light as cotton candy and her body felt as limp as the sheet draped over her.

6

Coffee cup in hand, Jessie crossed the porch and bent down to retrieve the *Narragansett Gazette*. Standing, she sipped her coffee and glanced at the paper. But, as she'd done for the past week, she found her thoughts drifting. Instead of seeing photos of the mayoral candidates, images of Nick flashed through her brain—of his dark head between her legs, of his tongue shooting spears of need over her stomach and to her breasts, making her body tremble. Her thighs had clenched with the urge to hold him to her, pull him closer, and prevent him from stopping.

Jessie was obsessed by Nick, by what he'd made her feel.

It felt like a spigot had been turned on. Decadent thoughts and feelings roiled around inside her, building and building, only to be blocked from release. Masturbation wasn't cutting it; she wasn't a one-night-stand kind of woman; and the kicker, she hadn't once thought of Martin, let alone missed him.

When you realize Martin can't give you what you need, let me know.

Who the hell was Nick? Why had he been in the backyard that night?

And most importantly, was he as good with his cock as his tongue and hands promised?

Shaking her head in disgust, she turned to make her way back into the house. The sudden roar of a car engine caused her to jerk around, which in turn caused hot java to slosh against her skin. But she barely noticed, her ears tuned in to a sound reminiscent of last week.

Her gaze latched on to the gleaming black Porsche Boxster pulling up into the front driveway of the house next door.

The driver's side door opened and closed.

A brown-haired man got out. He was dressed in jeans that hugged lean hips and a black T-shirt that couldn't hide his muscular shoulders.

Jessie blinked.

Dark glasses hid his eyes, but she'd be willing to bet they were brown. Her breath caught in her throat as he faced her dead-on.

Jessie forced regular breaths, attempting to stave off a bout of hyperventilation.

It was *him*.

His lips curved slightly, he nodded at her, and . . .

Jessie froze, willing him to step forward and walk over to her.

Instead, he turned away.

Disappointment flared deep in her stomach. She continued to stare, unable to look away, admiring the way the jeans hugged Nick's ass as he walked to the sign staked in the ground near the mailbox. He removed the "For Sale" portion of the sign.

"My new neighbor . . .?" she whispered.

Did that breathy voice just come out of her?

Oh. My. God.

Her heart did a somersault in her chest at the possibility that this exquisitely sculpted hunk might be her new neighbor.

Her pulse sang.

He wasn't a pervert, skulking around neighborhoods at night. He'd been in the yard because he'd bought the house. Well, he could be a homeowning pervert but—

Wait a minute. What if . . .

Nick continued to stand at the foot of the driveway, staring at the street as if waiting for someone.

. . . What if he was waiting for an SUV filled with a smiling wife and a vanload of energetic children?

Her heart took a nosedive for her stomach. She pulled her robe tighter around her and closed her eyes.

Please don't let a woman drive up. Surely Nick wouldn't have hinted at his abilities to satisfy her carnal needs if—Hell, forget hinted at. Surely he wouldn't lick and nibble her starving flesh if he was married with a family.

In this day and age, yes, he very well would.

Jessie opened her eyes.

Nick lifted a hand . . .

Jessie held her breath.

. . . to flag a moving truck.

The breath exploded from her lungs. Her heart returned to her chest. As Nick turned and walked up the driveway, he looked her way.

Long and hard.

Maybe images of being in her bed flitted through his brain. Maybe, behind those dark lenses, he was remembering her scent and taste and wanting more.

On impulse, Jessie lifted a hand and waved.

Once again, Nick nodded. After opening the garage, he disappeared inside.

Men in orange T-shirts and jeans unloaded the truck.

Jessie remained motionless, thinking. Okay, so Nick's response wasn't the most enthusiastic one she'd ever encountered. Especially after their last interaction. But, on the other hand, he had told her to come to him when she realized Martin couldn't give her what she needed.

Smiling, Jessie turned and scurried into the house.

Well, come to him she would, indeed.

7

Jessie mounted the last step and glanced inside the big bay window. Boxes seemed to cover every available inch of the living room, including the leather sofa and matching chair.

Her breath caught in her throat as her eyes rested on the man kneeling on the hardwood floor in front of the expensive entertainment center. Gone was the black T-shirt, giving her an excellent view of the masculine back and muscles that rippled as he fiddled with, well, whatever he was fiddling with.

He could be plucking strands of lint from between the knobs of the stereo for all she cared. All that interested her at the moment was the play of his deltoids as he moved, the flawless skin that looked as smooth as marble, the—

Suddenly, he stood, jerking her out of her trance.

She turned away and hurried to the door before he could turn around and catch her gaping at him. She tugged nervously on the hem of her dress. She was a novice at seduction.

What if he was no longer interested in her? What if she couldn't seduce him?

Take charge.

Be bold.
Do it.
Go sin.

Jessie rang the bell. As she waited for him to answer, she fluffed the tissue paper lining the basket she carried and straightened the bow on the handle.

A few seconds later, the door opened and she got a frontal view of his lust-provoking chest. Well, what little she could see out of the corner of her eyes. After all, staring and drooling at his chest would spoil the cool, in-control image she was shooting for.

She willed her gaze to remain fixed on his face, to not inch downward and explore the light coating of hair that dusted his chest, to not see if his jeans molded his hips like she suspected they did. Instead, she stared directly into his eyes. Eyes that were dark brown, just as she'd remembered, but without the warmth she'd seen when he'd looked up at her from between her legs.

Today, his eyes seemed to regard her politely.

Oh, God. Had he changed his mind?

Jessie gave him what she hoped was a dazzling smile—friendly, sexy, and interested all in one. "Hi. Since it looks like we're going to be neighbors, I wanted to welcome you to the neighborhood and introduce myself . . ."

She changed the tone of her voice, going for what she hoped was a throaty purr.

". . . properly. I'm Jessie Anderson."

She stuck out her hand.

His gaze flicked from her eyes to her hand, before once again returning to her face. The trip seemed to have changed his eye color from a soft brown to mocha.

Ahh, it looked like he was definitely warming up.

Finally, he grasped her hand, his strong, lean fingers completely engulfing her own. Once again, her body registered that these were *not* the pampered hands of a man who created spreadsheets all day, but rather, the functional hands of a man who used them.

A thrill shot through her at the slight roughness.

A pang of disappointment whizzed through her when he dropped her hand.

Jessie held the basket out to him. "Well, then . . . welcome to the neighborhood."

His eyes flicked to the basket, which he regarded with the same intensity as he'd regarded her fingers. After a few seconds, he took it from her.

"Thank you," he said.

Jessie smiled. "You're welcome."

She watched him rake a hand through his hair as he uttered a frustrated sigh. "Come in. We need to talk."

Talk?

Jessie frowned. Talking was not exactly what she had in mind. And since every man she'd ever known looked forward to serious conversation about as much as they relished having their chest hairs plucked with tweezers, "we need to talk" did not bode well.

She stood where she was.

He moved to the side.

With a shrug, she followed him into the house.

8

Nick knew that the last thing in the world he should do was invite Jessie into his house. Each morning, for the last seven days, he'd woken up with a hard-on and the memory of her juices teasing his taste buds.

He'd told her to contact him when she'd gotten rid of Martin.

Instead, she stood in front of him as a delegate from the Neighborhood Welcome Committee.

Her tousled black hair called to his fingers, her full lips glistened, begging him to devour their ripeness. His eyes took in every centimeter of her curvy body—which the simple dress erotically accentuated—to her painted toenails. Fire-engine red. He wanted to take each toe in his hands, gently spread them apart and suck until—

This was exactly the reason why he should have accepted her cookies, slammed the door behind her, and returned to tuning his amps.

Jessie made him feel lust when he didn't want to feel anything. He *couldn't* feel anything.

She was another man's woman.

His lips twisted—*Martin's* woman. Despite the fact that Martin was a dud in bed—Nick knew this because he'd barely gotten started when her body had quaked and quivered in his hands—he was not going to commit another wrong and finish what he'd started.

Even though his cock wanted to.

He turned and led the way to the kitchen, wanting to put some physical distance between her tempting body and his over-stimulated cock. Pushing aside a cardboard box of dishes sitting on the countertop, he sat the basket beside the box.

"I hope you have a sweet tooth. I made them myself."

Great. Not only did she taste good, she could bake. He ignored the goodies in the basket, looking at her instead. Plump lips. Plump breasts. Round hips. Goodies much more succulent than those resting between a bunch of twigs.

Damn.

"Look, we need to talk," he said.

"Let's have a snack first."

Images of his last "snack" with her zoomed through his mind—legs caressing his cheeks while his tongue had tasted her wetness, sampling the musky flavor that made him crave more.

He blinked. "Snack?"

"The basket," she prompted, her tone slightly amused, her bright eyes seemingly innocent.

Nick felt his face grow warm. He had to get these thoughts out of his mind. Shit, one would think he was starved for sex by the way he was acting—which was far from the truth. He had an active—albeit empty—sex life. But there was something about the dichotomy—the sexy vixen at odds with the girl-next-door freshness—that threw him off balance.

He snorted inwardly. *She is the girl next door.*

Okay. Food. Food would help him focus. Nick peered inside the basket and parted the tissue paper. He stared at the contents.

His cock twitched.

She laughed. A throaty, husky sound that belonged in the bedroom.

"I know they're a little juvenile, but I love bears," she said.

Nick lifted one of the bear cookies from the basket, noting the two-piece bathing suit that had been painted in red icing. Visions of just how much she loved bears flitted through his mind, of last week's bear getting to lick and lave the body he'd been denied, the sweet wetness he'd barely tasted. Pushing those images from his mind, he raised his gaze to Jessie's.

Merriment, with a hint of mischief, sparkled in her brown eyes.

Against his will, his gaze once again flicked over the "v" of her top. In his mind he stripped it from her body, seeing her breasts teasing him in the sheer red lingerie, breasts that the stuffed bear had "kissed." Breasts that he had kissed. Until she'd discovered he wasn't Martin.

His jaw tightened. He dropped the bear in the basket and pushed it away, returning his gaze to hers. "Look, I'm sorry about last week. What I did was wrong—"

"It didn't feel wrong," purred the sexy vixen.

He ignored the silky tone and the seductive smile curving her lips, instead focusing on the words he had to say. "Well, it *was* wrong and I—"

"Do you have anything to drink?"

What the hell was going on here? He was trying to talk and she wanted something to drink?

Nick frowned.

Jessie's shrug seemed apologetic. "I'm thirsty."

"Uh, tap water and maybe a bottle of wine. Somewhere."

"Wine sounds good."

Wine was the nectar of seduction. Not the drinking of the wine, but rather, watching Jessie's lips brush the rim of the glass instead of his lips or his neck or . . . his cock.

Wine sounded *really* good.

Enough of this. They were going to talk.

"Where's Martin?" His voice was harsher than he'd planned.

Jessie drew back. "Martin?"

Her tongue darted out, drawing his eyes to its movement as the pink flesh slid over the corner of her lip before hiding in her mouth. The gesture seemed to be made out of nervousness, not eroticism, but he still found the movement sensual. He wanted to nibble the moist flesh and suckle the soft tongue before thrusting into its wet hiding place.

"Um . . . Martin's gone."

Thoughts of Sandy came unbidden to his mind. When he'd caught up with the lies and called her on them, she'd shrugged and said, "Those men don't mean anything to me, Nicky. I love *you*." Was Jessie planning to dupe Martin and entice Nick to become one of the men who "didn't mean anything" to her?

"So you thought you'd come over here and 'play'?" While the cat was away and all that.

She grinned. "Yeah."

His jaw clenched. It shouldn't bother him, but it did. He'd wanted to believe that she was different, that the girl-next-door freshness meant goodness that went beyond the surface. But, while he'd been feeling remorse for his actions, she'd been intent on compounding the wrong.

Well, it doesn't bother your cock. Go ahead and "play" with her.

Nick returned his attention to Jessie.

Her smile disappeared. Her gaze became uncertain seconds before understanding seemed to dawn. "Oh. I meant Martin's *gone*, as in out of my life. I broke up with him."

Nick's anger subsided. Relief took its place. Jessie's news flash changed things—if it was true, that is. "Why?"

She frowned. "Does it really matter why?"

Yes, it mattered. Especially if Martin didn't realize it was over and was going to come banging on his door.

He shrugged. "Last week, you were trying to seduce him. This week, you're seducing me."

"Am I? Seducing you?"

Hell, yeah. Her lidded eyes and plump lips sent another rush of blood to his groin.

He shifted, trying to relieve a bit of pressure.

"Didn't you tell me to call you when I realized that Martin couldn't give me what I needed? Well . . ." She licked her lower lip. ". . . I'm calling you."

Thank you, God. She was not representing the Neighborhood Welcome Committee.

Her words were a dream come true. A *wet* dream come true. She wanted him. She was available. She was accessible. Hell, she lived next door—

Ah, shit. He hadn't been thinking with the big head when he'd told her to come to him. The fact was that they were neighbors and, after the sex was gone, they'd still be neighbors. The needs he'd been referring to were strictly the physical, you-come-I-come kind of needs. Nothing more.

He'd said the words because they'd popped into his mind—and, if he were honest, his ego had gotten the better of him. He'd been feeling superior, filled with lust and bravado because he'd been satisfying her in ways Martin never had. He'd figured she'd eventually dump the inept Martin, but he'd never thought she'd do it this soon.

Had she broken up with Martin because of what he'd said? Was she looking for a relationship?

Damn. He hadn't been *thinking* at all.

"Is there a problem?" she asked.

Hell, no. No problem here, his cock urged.

He raised a brow. "Rebounding?"

She laughed.

He waited.

"No," she said after the laughter died. "I'm not rebounding. To rebound, there has to be something to rebound from. Martin and I were over long before you . . . showed up. That night was an irrational attempt to postpone the inevitable. Today is a rational attempt to have some fun."

Sounds good to me. "You just want fun?"

"Yes." She looked him straight in the eyes.

Okay. She wanted him. She wanted sex. She didn't want the big R—a relationship.

His conscience was happy.

"So . . . are you going to satisfy my . . ." Her tongue made another appearance between her lips. ". . . thirst."

"Are you sure you're thirsty?"

Her gaze dropped, seemingly focused on his mouth. Her smile slipped. Her eyes darkened.

His cock lengthened.

"Oh, yes. Very thirsty," she said.

Her sultry purr suddenly left his throat parched. He was very thirsty, too.

Let the thirst-quenching begin.

"Well, then . . ." Nick smiled and turned, rummaging through a nearby box. He was going to drag this out, switch the roles, and leave her off balance. "Voila," he said, his hand circling the desired item. "Merlot. Red wine goes with red dishes." He sat the bottle on the countertop with a flourish.

Jessie burst out laughing. No braying sound to this laugh. Rather, a sultry purr that penetrated his skin and circulated through his blood stream, raising his temperature by ten degrees.

Or, was that twenty?

He ignored its effect.

For the moment.

She picked up a bear clad in red boxer shorts. "Then I'm glad I brought the red dish."

"Me, too." Only he wasn't talking about red bear cookies. Instead, he was imagining her body as he'd last seen it, blazing hot underneath the red robe, nipples hard and begging to be tasted.

She blushed, her lowered gaze implying that she'd read his mind.

He grinned. "Make yourself at home while I look for glasses." His gaze scanned the stacks of boxes. "This may take a while," he finished wryly.

He watched her turn and stroll towards the living room, his need no longer masked as he stared at her ass, seeing the firm cheeks she'd cupped between her fingers.

He forced the enticing picture out of his mind and turned his attention back to the task at hand. He tore open a second box and prayed that he'd find glasses inside. God must've been listening, for not only were there glasses, but a corkscrew as well. He whispered a thanks as he swept the wine, corkscrew, glasses, and basket from the counter, then grabbed a roll of paper towels and headed for the living room.

His eyes immediately went to Jessie as she squatted in front of the CD rack.

"You have quite a CD collection," she said over her shoulder.

He watched a red-tipped nail, at odds with her current Susie Homemaker image, lightly skip over the CDs.

"Luther Vandross, Kenny G, Uncle Kracker..." she recited, standing.

He placed everything on the coffee table and joined her in

front of the CD stand. He smiled and stopped behind her, invading her space. "Yeah, I like a little bit of everything." His breath stirred her hair.

Did she shrug or was that a shiver?

Reaching around her, he intentionally brushed her arm as he reached for a CD. The buzz that went through him momentarily distracted him. Jessie jumped, obviously affected just as he had been.

Ahhh. The sexy siren wasn't as calm and collected as she pretended to be. So, his breath must've caused a shiver.

He smiled and resumed his search, stopping at the Fourplay CD. "Have you heard this one before?"

"No. Fourplay? What is it?" she asked.

The tremor in her voice pleased him. More than pleased him. Excited him. He fought the urge to slip his hands under her skirt and around her waist, before pulling her hips back and rubbing her ass against his cock.

Instead, he reached around her and opened the CD changer. Their bare arms once again brushed, sending another jolt through him.

"Let me show you," he whispered in her ear.

9

Jessie forced her breathing to remain even, normal, as Nick reached around her. The heat from his chest seemed to burn her back through her thin cotton shirt. And he wasn't even touching her. She imagined what she'd feel if she leaned back a fraction of an inch, leaning into the hardness of his chest.

And she knew it would be hard. She could tell by the way his muscles flexed when he moved. The same muscles that she'd been trying to ignore since she'd walked in here.

She jumped when his arm touched hers again as he opened the CD changer. What was wrong with her? The man had just barely brushed against her and she wanted to grab his arms and grind her body along the hard length of him. She had to get her body under control. Otherwise, her plan to seduce him—to drive *him* wild—would end in embarrassment.

She wanted to appear sexy and seductive, not desperate.

With a start, she realized he'd been talking to her.

"I'm sorry. What did you say? I . . . was listening to this CD."

His laugh rumbled behind her. Deep. Low. Sexy. "I asked you what you thought of the music."

Jessie tuned in to the music, listening for the first time, trying to ignore Nick's hips that were mere inches away. A male voice crooned some ballad about waiting for love. His problems sounded trivial to her, compared to the battle of desire going on inside her.

She struggled to come up with something seductive.

"It's aptly named," she said, dropping her voice to a husky rasp. "The music pulses with energy that caresses the skin and strokes the soul, making the body want to move in . . . hard . . . slow . . . movements . . ."

Did she hear him draw a shaky breath?

"Great description." His voice was hoarse.

Eureka!

Jessie smiled as he stepped away from her. Maybe she was better at seduction than she thought.

She turned around and faced Nick.

"Have a seat," he said as he moved a box out of the way.

As she sat down on the couch, she watched him work the cork out of the bottle and sink into the leather chair opposite her.

Damn.

She'd hoped he'd take a seat next to her. Kind of hard to run her fingers along his arm or down his chest from ten feet away.

Time to come up with plan B.

While he reached for a cookie, her eyes roamed greedily over his chest, down to where the waistband of his jeans met his tight abdomen. Mingled with her blatant lust was a stab of envy. It wasn't fair that he could lean over without displaying a trace of flab. She had to spend hours on the Lifecycle for every ounce of muscle she possessed.

She averted her eyes hastily as he leaned back in his chair, long legs sprawled out in front of him, carelessly parted in a "v."

He munched on a cookie, then said, "Mmmmm. These are great. I think I've acquired a love of bears as well."

The slight emphasis on the word "bears" made Jessie wonder if he was referring to Teddy, the way she had slid the stuffed bear across her abdomen and over her pussy.

Her face felt warm, pleasantly warm.

She leaned back against the couch and stretched.

Nick's gaze dropped to her breasts.

Jessie smiled. "I'm glad you like my bears." She lowered her hands, moving one to her breast, tracing the edge of her top with a fingertip. "So what should we do next, Nick? Get to know each other?"

Nick's smile seduced while his eyes followed the movement of her fingertip. "Two people getting to know each other is always good."

She traced her cleavage.

Nick licked his lips.

"Okay . . ."

She slid her fingers under her top, caressing her flesh, nearing her nipple.

". . . What brings you to Narragansett?"

"I'm buying a commercial building in Providence . . . Narragansett is close. This is a great house . . ." He sounded distracted.

Jessie forced her eyes away from his, ignoring the heat in his gaze, letting her gaze circle the room instead.

She smiled. "Yes, this is a great house. It's got great windows." She pointed to the bay window she'd observed him through earlier. "That one is perfect for . . . entertaining."

She turned back to Nick. He held the wineglass by the stem, idly swirling the red wine, looking as if his mind was elsewhere.

And, if she judged the smoky gleam in his eyes correctly, his mind was definitely elsewhere.

Probably, rolling around in the gutter with hers.

His lips quirked and he inclined his head slightly. "Is that what you came over here for? To entertain me?"

"No. I did not come over to entertain, Nick."

He took a sip of wine.

She watched his mouth as he drank the wine. His mouth. Her body flooded with remembrance. She wanted his mouth back—on her, not on some stupid wineglass.

Jessie picked up a bear cookie with polka-dot boxers. She sucked lightly on the bear's leg.

Nick's smile slipped.

"I came over to play, Nick . . ." She removed the cookie from her mouth, licking the bear instead, letting her tongue outline the foot and leg, stopping at the "v" between its legs.

Nick's gaze was riveted on her mouth.

Jessie's gaze was riveted on his mouth, to the tongue that peeked out between his lips as he licked them lightly.

She swallowed hard.

"What game did you have in mind?" he asked.

Her mind scrambled to think, for she hadn't been *thinking* of anything. Instead, she'd been *feeling*—feeling heat begin to spread through her body at the sight of the sexual haze that seemed to cloud his gaze. And, as the heat spread, growing hotter, traveling faster, the harder it became to think of something.

No, playing games was the last thing that had been on her mind when she'd showed up on his doorstep. And, now, the only game she wanted to play, was one that involved the two of them naked, their bodies touching, their hands stroking, satisfying the ache that was growing stronger and stronger within her—

Ache . . . Games . . .

Jessie bit off the bear's leg and smiled. "Doctor."

"Huh?"

Apparently, she wasn't the only one having trouble thinking.

Nick raised his gaze from her lips to her eyes, and blinked, as if trying to focus.

"I came over to play 'Doctor.'"

Lightbulbs did not appear to be going off behind his eyes. In fact, his eyes had that hooded look that implied his thoughts were sexual, still on the action of her lips on the bear cookie, possibly imagining her lips on him, kissing, nibbling, joined by the swirl of her tongue and—

Her breath caught in her throat. She forced it out lightly. "Surely you played 'Doctor' when you were a kid?"

"No."

"Well. That seems positively un-American."

"I guess I'm deprived." His smile was sly. "So un-deprive me. I'm ready to play."

He reached for another cookie. Jessie watched his teeth encircle the bikini-clad bear, taking an almost delicate bite.

That was odd. There was nothing about Nick that was dainty or delicate. Then she noticed where he'd taken the bite.

He'd eaten the crotch.

Her eyes snapped to his, catching the devilish glint behind the sexy stare.

"Show me," he said softly.

10

Heat rushed to her pussy at the thought of showing Nick how to play "Doctor." Jessie ignored her body's response, determined to drag things out, to tease Nick—and herself. Striving to remain as nonchalant as he appeared to be, she picked up the wineglass.

"I'm the doctor and you're the patient. First, we'll need . . ."

She ran her fingertip lightly around the rim before dipping it into the dark liquid. Lifting her wine-coated finger to her lips, her tongue darting out, lightly licking the tip, before suckling it with a kisslike movement. All the while, she stared directly into Nick's eyes, watching his eyes darken as he watched her.

". . . medicine."

She made a big production of sipping the wine, raising the glass slowly to her lips, taking a leisurely sip, letting it linger in her mouth just a bit, before swallowing noticeably.

Nick watched the intoxicating liquid slide down her throat, with what appeared to be envy.

She smiled and tilted the glass. "Yes, I think that this will do." She stood. "Next, we'll need an examining table."

Nick popped up from the chair and rushed to the dining-room, nearly flinging the boxes off the table.

When the table was cleared, he turned to her, his expression eager. "Will this do?"

She hid a grin. "Yes. Now you need to hop up on the table and lie down."

He swung himself up and lay on his back, near the edge.

Jessie stepped forward, stopping next to him and setting the glass on the tabletop. "Now, I need to examine you, see if you have any hurts that I can fix."

"Doctor, I'm in great pain."

She met his gaze. Anticipation, not pain, shone in his eyes, proving him to be a lousy actor.

Jessie's lips twitched. "Yes, I can see that." She ran her fingers over his shoulders. "I bet you hurt here . . ." She trailed her fingertips over his chest, circling his areola, pinching his nipples.

He inhaled sharply. "Yes."

". . . and here . . ." She trailed her fingers over his abdomen.

His stomach rippled. "Yes."

"You hurt from all that heavy lifting you did today."

"Yes."

She retraced the path of her fingers. "Kisses always make the pain a little less."

"That might make the pain a little worse," he said, his gaze locked on the movement of her hand.

Jessie smiled. "Sometimes it has to hurt before it gets better. About the pain here . . ." She leaned forward and placed her lips against his collarbone, kissing and tracing it with her tongue, before moving upward. She sucked and licked the muscle that ran from his neck to his shoulder.

Nick moved his head to the side, giving her better access.

"Feel better?" she asked.

"No," he said between gritted teeth.

While suckling his neck, she let her hands wander over his chest, palms caressing his pecs. She felt his nipples turn into hard nubs under her flesh.

He inhaled sharply.

"Feel better now?"

Nick remained silent.

She trailed her tongue over his chest, flicking his nipples, before moving down to his abdomen.

His stomach quivered.

She dipped her fingers under the waistband of his jeans, her palm resting on his cock. "Hmmm . . . I notice a bit of swelling here."

She raised her head from his stomach and traced his waist with her fingertips.

His cock traced his zipper.

"It's very swollen," he said.

"Yes. And it looks very, very painful," she said throatily.

"It is." His voice was hoarse. "I need release."

She gave him a disapproving stare. "Release, Mr. Ralston?"

"Oh . . . Uh . . . I meant, relief. I need relief."

Judging by the way his voice cracked, he did sound like a man in need. And judging by the way his eyes blazed, he looked like a man in dire need of what she could give him.

"Yes, you do," she said.

Using both hands, Jessie unbuttoned the top button on his jeans. "I'm going to have to take off your jeans to get a closer look at your condition, Mr. Ralston. Do you mind?"

"No. Please."

"I must warn you. We ran out of hospital gowns."

"That's fine, that's fine. I just need—"

"Relief. I understand, Mr. Ralston."

She unzipped his jeans, her eyes glued to the ever-growing bulge beneath her touch.

Ever helpful, Nick lifted his hips.

Jessie tugged the jeans over them, then hooked her fingers in the sides of his briefs and repeated the downward motion.

"Why, Mr. Ralston, I don't believe I've met a patient so eager to assist in—"

As his cock cleared the cotton, the words died in her throat and her heart slammed in her chest.

"Wow," she breathed.

Despite the male obsession with size, she'd never paid much attention to it, believing that how a man used his cock—not the size of it—was what mattered.

It was easy to disregard size when she'd never had to consider it before. But looking at the cock pointing towards Nick's navel, she decided that maybe she'd discounted size prematurely. For size gave a woman additional options—if the man didn't know what to do with it, the woman did. After all, she was a master with her dildo, and Nick seemed to be at least as big.

But she'd be willing to bet he'd know what to do with his natural . . . gift. Surely someone with such skill with his mouth and tongue—

"Is there a problem, Doctor?"

"Ooooh, no—no problem here." She sounded breathless.

Nick's chuckle was strained.

Jessie continued pulling downward, until his underwear joined his jeans around his ankles.

"Yes, yes, I can see why you were in pain. There appears to be extreme rigidity . . . ." She wrapped her hand around his cock.

The breath hissed out of him.

"Did that hurt?"

"Oh, yeah."

Oh, God. He felt so good in her hand. His skin was so smooth, his cock was so hard. She wanted to climb onto the table and straddle his hips and—

"Is there a cure?" His tone was urgent.

"I . . . I think s-so." Her voice trembled. Jessie cleared the lust from her throat. "We're going to have to try multiple treatments."

"Okay."

"First, we're going to try a . . . therapeutic massage." She moved her hand up his shaft.

Nick moaned.

She stopped. "Is that too painful, Mr. Ralston?"

"No." His hand gripped hers, moving it down his cock.

She jerked her hand away. "I am the doctor and you are the patient. Do I have to buckle your hands down onto the examining table?" Her attempt to be stern failed.

She sounded aroused.

He let his hands fall to the side. "Sorry, Doctor." His attempt at contrition failed.

He sounded impatient.

Jessie pressed her lips together to contain her smile. Once again, she wrapped her hand around his cock. She moved it down to the base, her wrist touching his balls.

He thrust his hips up.

She moved her hand up, burying the head of his cock in her palm.

He yanked his hips down.

His movement was frantic, inciting her passion, igniting her need. Her breathing was ragged.

"Y-you seem to be c-crazed by pain. I think you need a painkiller. Open your m-mouth."

He did as instructed.

Her hand shook as she reached for the glass. She dipped her forefinger into the wine and touched his tongue.

He licked her finger, swirling his tongue around the tip and up the sides, before closing his lips around it. His mouth felt hot and moist.

He sucked and licked.

Jessie gasped. God, the man was good with his mouth.

His cock fucked her hand.

His mouth fucked her finger.

Jessie's body thrummed with need.

Suddenly, Nick turned his head to the side, dislodging her finger, and gripped her hands, stilling her stroking of his cock. "No," he said between gritted teeth.

Jessie stilled.

Nick stilled.

His ragged breathing filled the air. "You're a lousy doctor," he said finally. "My pain is worse than when you started."

Jessie feigned a hurt expression. "Well, if you feel that way . . ." She let go of his cock and slid her hands from under his, then drew back, intent on moving away.

Nick sat up and swung his legs to the side of the table. He kicked his jeans and briefs from around his ankles and stood. Putting his hands on her thighs, he pulled her to him. His hands caressed her skin, making their way under the hem of her skirt.

Nick's breath hissed out of him, ending on a curse. "You aren't wearing panties?"

"A doctor comes prepared for action."

Nick made a strangled sound in the back of his throat. His hand moved to the nape of her neck, pulling her forward, bringing her mouth to his.

As her lips touched his, all thoughts of their game went out of her mind. His lips were so soft. Her mouth parted under his and she strained forward, coaxing them wider with her tongue, desperate for a taste. Her heart doubled its beat, her breathing accelerated. Slipping her hand to the base of his neck, she pulled his head closer. Slanting her head, she took the kiss deeper.

Nick's hands massaged and stroked her shoulders, before moving down her back. His other hand joined the action. Up and down, his hands moved restlessly over her.

Nick broke the kiss, his breath rasping in his throat.

Jessie opened her eyes—when had she closed them?—in time to see his head lower, in time to feel his lips on her throat. He kissed, inhaling at the same time, creating a cooling sensation that heated her skin.

Jessie shivered.

"You seem to have pain, too," he whispered against her neck, the warm air heating her flesh just as the cool air had done. He trailed his tongue along her shoulder, tracing the path her fingers had made when she'd pointed out his pain, going lower, across the swell of her breasts accessible above the neckline of her dress.

"N-no, I'm fine," she lied, remembering the game, struggling to get it back on track, despite the very real "pain" inflamed by his tongue.

She drew back.

He pulled her forward, and bent down, his mouth capturing a nipple through the cloth.

"Oh!" she cried.

His mouth suckled.

Sensation careened through her body, sparked by the simple action of his moist mouth searing her through the thin material, his firm hands massaging her tense body.

Jessie pulled her chest back, wanting him to pull the cotton away from her skin and take her flesh in his mouth. She pressed her hips forward and upward, using the friction to quell some of the need surging through her.

Nick tightened his grip on her hips and pivoted. The next thing she knew, Jessie found herself sitting on the table. "What are you doing?"

His hands strummed her back, seeking, searching, finding her zipper on the back of her top. He pulled it down. "Putting you on the examining table."

"The doctor belongs on the other side of the table."

He slid the straps of her top over her shoulders and off her hands. The halter top pooled around her waist. Her nipples instantly hardened under his stare.

Nick lifted his gaze to hers. His eyes blazed with want. His lips curved into a smile. "I think I understand how this game works. I'm the doctor now."

11

Before Jessie could respond, his mouth returned to her breast, his flesh touching her flesh, just as she'd tried to urge him to do in the living room.

"Is that where it hurts?" he asked, his voice muffled by the nipple he teased with his tongue.

Jessie moaned and her hands tightened on his shoulders. This time, her hold on him wasn't for fear of falling but, rather, for fear that he'd move away, that he'd stop swirling his tongue, which would put an end to the delicious tingles sparking from her chest, dipping into her stomach, dropping lower to the lips swollen with want.

Her thighs guided him closer.

He leaned forward and while his mouth continued teasing her breasts, his body forced her backward.

Jessie removed her hands from Nick's shoulders and used her elbows to ease her descent onto the tabletop.

The glass tabletop felt hard and cold under her back. Nick's tongue felt soft and hot against her skin.

She placed her hands to his head, pressing him closer, guiding him to the left, then right, coercing him to apply more pressure.

"Is this where it hurts?" he repeated, warming her nipple with his breath. "Or . . . ?"

He grabbed her hips and pulled her down to the edge of the table. His cock nudged her pussy. "Or here?"

She gasped. Jessie arched her back, pushing her nipple deeper into his throat. "Yes, it hurts there."

She gripped his hips tightly with her thighs. His cock nestled against her pussy.

She groaned.

He moaned.

"And there, too. You need to make it better . . . now!" She pressed forward for emphasis.

While his mouth worked its magic on her skin—from one nipple to the next, laving and tasting, to her throat, past her shoulder, finally returning to her mouth—his fingers slid between their bodies, guiding what she wanted most to where she most wanted it.

His cock hovered inside her pussy lips. "Is this what you wanted?"

Jessie thrust her hips forward, pushing him inside her.

He cursed.

She cried.

His hips pumped.

Her hands gripped, pulling him closer, greedy for more—more flesh against flesh, more flesh inside flesh, more feeling, more sensation. Awe and desire swirled inside her. Awe because while Nick had barely fondled her body, he'd ignited her passion. His words, the intensity of his focus—as if she where the only woman who mattered—the tease of his touch, served as mental foreplay, which inflamed her body with physical want.

Martin's touch had been functional, an act performed seemingly because it was required.

Nick's touch was reverent, an act performed for mutual enjoyment.

Martin's lovemaking had been silent, as if noise would break his concentration, impede satisfaction.

Nick's lovemaking was vocal. His breath flung noisily from his lungs. He gasped. He grunted. He whispered words of encouragement—"Oh, God, I like that." He whispered words of praise—"You feel so good."

Martin was controlled, his touch light, his movements rhythmic and predictable.

Nick was spontaneous. His hands gripped and clutched. His body quivered and jerked.

Martin took, coming before she'd been satisfied, leaving her to resort to manual stimulation afterwards.

Nick gave. His mouth moved over hers, stoking her passion. His body pressed against hers—his heart beat in sync with hers, his breathing merged with hers. His hips where like pistons, driving into her, driving her need higher.

The heat burning inside her became too much to hold. She dug her heels into Nick's ass, and her fingernails into his back, as the passion he'd kindled inside spilled outward.

She screamed.

Nick groaned.

Her body quaked.

Nick's body tensed. His fingers clutched. His cock jerked and spasmed deep inside her.

Time became meaningless, as her total awareness hung on the riotous sensation exploding within her body . . .

As her heart rate returned to normal and Nick's erratic breathing subsided, the final comparison flitted through her mind:

With Martin, Jessie had felt distant.

With Nick, she felt connected.

How in the hell had that happened?

12

As Nick's breathing returned to normal, he realized Jessie was supporting more of his body than he was. He shifted, transferring this weight from her chest to his forearms, resting alongside her shoulders. He brushed his lips against the side of her neck, tasting the slight saltiness dotting her skin.

Saltiness because of his touch, his kiss, his sex.

His cock stirred inside her. He grinned inwardly. Again? Maybe his cock was thinking about more action, but there was no time. He had a flight to catch in a few hours.

Which was too bad because sex had been incredible. Never before had fucking been fun. Sex with Sandy had been serious, intense, making him feel like they were in some sort of competition. Maybe he was competing, considering all the other men that had been in the race without his knowledge.

With Jessie, he was able to take risks, to be imaginative and silly. In short, to be himself. Whatever he felt like being at the moment.

Playful. Naughty. Goofy.

What a novel concept—feeling free to be himself during sex.

With a woman who was equally free and fun and silly and naughty.

Very, very, naughty.

He smiled at the thought.

Not wanting to crush Jessie, he pushed his hips away and pulled out of her.

His cock was free.

The connection remained.

Nick glanced at Jessie's face. As if suddenly aware of his gaze, the dreaminess—mixed with something resembling fear—that seemed to flicker in her eyes, was instantly masked. A smile curved her lips and her gaze dropped to the vicinity of his nose.

He recognized the look he'd glimpsed. It was a look that said that the woman under him or on top of him or across from him was feeling more than sex, but trying to hide it.

Or maybe that was just wishful thinking on his part.

It didn't feel like wishful thinking—hell, he didn't even understand why he was wishing for it, given his vow to avoid women. Well, now, he was making a slight correction to the vow.

He was going to avoid the *wrong* type of woman.

And, so far, Jessie felt like the right type.

And speaking of type, he also knew she was the relationship type—he'd known that the night he'd ended up in her bedroom, when she'd cried out for Martin. Just as he'd known that, after being aroused by her naked body in the window, after hearing her throaty plea, after finding himself between her legs, sampling her juices, tasting her need—

His cock lengthened, caressing her thigh and sending a jolt of lust up to his stomach.

That night, he'd desperately wanted to be Martin.

"You okay?" she asked.

Funny question. It was the one *he* usually asked. "Yeah."

"Good."

Her gaze returned to his. All traces of vulnerability had disappeared, replaced by a look completely feline. Her legs slid up and down his ass, her clit brushed up against his cock.

"The doctor seems to still be in the house," she purred.

Nick laughed.

Jessie grinned.

"You want more?" he asked.

Her heels once again dug into his ass, urging him closer. "Oh, yeah."

"All right." He laughed again, appreciating the irony that this was the first time he could remember in a long while that he didn't need it again—though he definitely wanted it—while the woman he was with did.

Maybe he'd have to take a later flight.

Jessie's fingertips circled his cock and wiped all thoughts of travel plans from his mind. And as her fingers guided him back to where she wanted him, and as her hips tilted forward, positioning him at the wet entrance she wanted him to enter, he forgot that he was satisfied.

Lust slammed through him.

His hips slammed against hers, thrusting his cock inside her.

She gasped.

He grunted.

And everything became mindless, every action became instinctual.

Her hips, undulating underneath his, set the pace, making him drive into her faster, then slower, then deeper, then more shallow.

Her voice, chanting his name in breathless spurts, pleaded and demanded at the same time, telling him what she needed.

He gripped her ass, holding her still, and she moaned his

name; he plundered her mouth, sucked her neck, bit her nipple, and his name slipped from her lips like a shiver; he said her name, urging her onward and upward, and she obliged.

Her body jerked against his.

His name exploded from her mouth, barely decipherable.

Released from her need, Nick was free to go after his own. He pumped furiously.

He held her closer and tighter, needing the heat from her body to merge with his.

He covered her mouth with his, catching her jerky breath, needing the air sustaining her to sustain him.

His body tensed. His cock pulsed.

And all the heat that had been building in his body, erupted inside hers, leaving him shuddering at the loss.

Oddly, that orgasm was better than the first—stronger, more intense, longer-lasting. On a scale of one to ten, definitely a twelve.

"Wow. That was . . . fun," she said.

Using what little air remained in his lungs, Nick laughed.

Jessie frowned as Nick's laughter rumbled through her, as his breath bounced off of her shoulder. "What's so funny?"

"Fun? That's it? Please. Don't stroke my ego so."

Jessie smiled. "I'll have you know, that is a major compliment. It was also awesome, spectacular, sinful . . ."

"Okay, okay." Still laughing, Nick pulled out of her and moved away. "I was just teasing you. That was my word for it as well. One of my words anyway."

She kept her smile in place, struggling between wanting to know what other words he would use to describe what had just happened and wondering if his abrupt departure signaled the end of their rendezvous. She watched him pick up his jeans and walk to the stereo and flick a switch.

Lite jazz filled the room.

Nervousness filled her. She yawned, then stretched.

This was why she never engaged in casual sex. She never knew what the rules were afterwards.

Well, that was only one reason.

The main reason was probably because she felt there were no guarantees that sex would be any good—and what could be more humiliating than having sex for sex's sake and having it be *bad* sex?

Well, she definitely didn't need to worry about bad sex with Nick. Two orgasms in less than an hour. How had that happened?

It used to take Martin an hour to bring her to orgasm, and sometimes—out of embarrassment for both of them—she faked it. Not that Martin was bad in bed. He was just so . . . serious about sex. It was like, well, another audit he had to perform. He'd never go along with her need for play, for teasing.

Not like Nick.

All he'd had to do is nibble a few bear cookies, play a game or two of doctor, throw in a few smoky glances and hot touches, and a raging inferno had consumed her body.

Who would've thought fun could be such a powerful aphrodisiac?

She sat up, just as Nick, clad only in his half-zipped up jeans, returned and stopped in front of her.

Tissue touched her skin as he wiped the wetness from her thighs and higher. He pulled her dress down, covering the tops of her legs, then slid the straps of her top up her arms and over her shoulders. Reaching behind her, he zipped the back, leaving her fully covered as if he'd never touched her.

Only the comfortable ache and the remaining wetness in her pussy was a pleasant reminder of all that had happened.

Jessie sighed and slid from the table, looking around the

room for her sandals. She didn't even remember taking them off. They must be—

Nick took her hand in his and led her to the couch. He sat down and pulled her down onto his lap. "I would invite you into my bed, only I don't have one."

"How can you not have a bed?" she asked. "Seems like that's one of the most important pieces of furniture."

"Yeah, well, my ex-girlfriend thought so, too. Since everyone but me seemed to be in it, I decided to get a new one."

"Oh . . ." What did one say to that? "I'm sorry."

Nick rubbed her back and placed a light kiss on her forehead. "Don't be. I was over her a long time ago. I just didn't realize how long ago until last week."

Could he mean what she thought he meant? That meeting her had something to do with his realization?

Before she could think of a way to ask him, he changed the subject.

"I wish I could stay the night with you but I have to go."

"This late? Where?"

Too late, she caught herself. She barely knew him. Where he was going was none of her business. Hours of spectacular sex did not give her any right to answers.

Her face felt warm. "Oh, I mean, sure. No problem." She scrambled to get off his lap.

He held her down. "I have to catch a flight to New York— sign the papers on the house I sold."

Jessie relaxed, pleased that he'd told her.

"I'll be back late Sunday night. I'd like to see you."

Happiness welled up in her heart. "I'd like that, too. How about I leave a key out for you?"

"Under the flowerpot?"

"How'd you know?"

Nick laughed. "Because it sounds like you."

She drew back to look at him. "How's that?"

His expression was serious. "Honest, trusting."

"Yeah. I guess so." She lay her head on his chest. "Mmm. This feels nice . . . Let me know when you have to go."

They sat in silence.

He rubbed her back.

She stroked his arm.

Sitting with Nick felt so . . . nice, so comfortable.

Martin hadn't been big into cuddling, seeing it more as a duty than a delight. Nick seemed content, as if enjoying the feel of her, desiring her touch.

The music played softly in the background.

The silence grew between them.

And still, she felt comfortable.

An advertisement for *The Sin Club* interrupted her peace, forcing her to break the silence. "I was 'sinning' the day I met you."

"Hmmmm?" His voice was relaxed.

"I'd been listening to Dr. Love, taking his advice to be bold, to go for it, to 'sin.' He was right. If I hadn't done it, I wouldn't have met you."

"I'm glad you did . . . I guess I've sinned, too."

"What was your sin?"

"Deciding to take a chance with you."

13

Deciding to take a chance with you.

Nick's words had danced through her mind ever since they'd parted. The promise they held made her glow. She'd barely been able to concentrate, anxiously waiting for his return home.

And now it was Sunday. He'd be here shortly.

Jessie adjusted the pillow behind her back and sipped her wine, letting her gaze circle her bedroom. Her eyes lingered on the window and she smiled. It was hard to believe that one little striptease in this room had changed her life so drastically.

She took another sip of wine and let her gaze move on.

To Teddy, who she would never again think of as an innocent bear.

To her dresser where the red silk scarf sat that she'd used as a blindfold as she'd waited for Martin—

Jessie frowned as she took a gulp of Merlot. Speaking of Martin, he was supposed to have picked up his stuff today and hadn't showed. Not that she was surprised. When was the last time he'd followed through on a commitment he'd made?

Heck, he hadn't even opened her please-come-home-and-fuck-me invitation.

"He didn't think it was 'important,'" she muttered, bracketing the word "important" in the air with her fingers.

She giggled. "Yeah, well, Nick thought it was important. I gave him an invitation he couldn't resist." She giggled again, this time until tears sprang to her eyes. As the laughter ended, she reached for the bottle on her nightstand, and paused.

Maybe she shouldn't have any more to drink. Oh, one more glass. There was plenty left for Nick.

Or maybe not.

As she tilted the bottle over her glass, nothing came out. Damn. She set both the glass and the bottle on the nightstand. How had that happened? How had she managed to finish off the whole bottle?

Guess she was tipsier than she'd thought. Well, thank God Nick's plane was late. It'd give her some time to sober up and be alert and ready when he came in.

Nick.

Just the mention of his name made her body hot. The things they'd done—she'd never thought a child's game could be so erotic.

The things they were going to do . . .

Jessie slid under the covers and closed her eyes, letting her mind replay the surprise she'd planned for Nick. Another striptease.

Only, this time, instead of him standing outside her window, he'd be inside . . .

Nick sits on her bed. Wearing a smile and the same slinky red gown he'd first seen her in, Jessie strolls and struts in front of him, gyrating her hips and . . .

She burrowed deeper under the covers.

. . . running her hands down her body. She shimmies up to

him and, holding a breast in each hand, she bends to within centimeters of his mouth and lets her nipples graze his lips. Then, she stands and twirls around, giving him a view of her ass, before sitting on his lap . . .

Jessie yawned. Her body felt so tired . . .

. . . His cock is as hard as a rock behind the zipper of his pants. And, as she rubs her ass against him—up and down, side to side—he grows even harder. He wants to touch her, but he can't. He asks . . .

. . . asks . . .

. . . asks . . .

"Is it okay if I stay?" he whispered in her ear.

Jessie stirred, feeling an arm across her waist and a cock pressed against her ass. Nick's *hard* cock. She smiled and her eyes fluttered open, taking in the pitch black room, then drifted shut again.

She must've fallen asleep.

"You came," she said.

"Shhhh. Go back to sleep. We'll talk in the morning."

She didn't want to go back to sleep. She tried to open her eyes again. But she was sleepy. "Okay," she said, scooting back against Nick.

He gasped.

She smiled . . .

. . . asks, "Is it okay if I stay?"

She places her hands on his thighs for better leverage and rubs her ass against his cock harder, faster. "You're not going anywhere," she says.

His breath is ragged in her ear.

His chest is tense against her back.

"Do you want me, Nick?"

"Oh, God, yes."

She likes the pain of need she hears in his voice. It excites her, makes her feel feminine and powerful and desirable. But she's had enough of the games.

She wants him, too.

She rises and turns to face him, pulling him to his feet. Unbuttoning and unzipping his jeans, she pulls his jeans and underwear over his hips. Her body throbs at the sight of him.

As usual, he is ready for her.

She pushes him onto the bed and climbs on top of him and . . .

The bed dipped sharply to the right seconds before a loud crash yanked Jessie out of the dream. She shot straight up and turned around, facing the bedroom door.

Her mouth dropped open.

The hallway light illuminated Nick, standing in front of the closet door, completely naked, broken glass from the lamp on the floor in front of him.

Martin stood, wearing only a tank undershirt and black socks.

Jessie closed her eyes.

When she reopened her eyes, both men still stood naked in front of her.

What the hell was going on here?

"He kissed my neck," Martin yelled, scrubbing the back of his neck with his hand. "Jessie, give me the baseball bat."

"I'd love to give you the bat, Martin," she said, unmoving. "What are you—"

Totally missing her sarcasm, he held out his hand impatiently. "Well?"

Nick reached down to pick up his jeans.

"Nick, don't—"

"Don't move," said Martin to Nick. He ducked under the bed and picked up the bat. "Jessie, call the police."

Nick put on his jeans and bent to pick up his shirt.

Martin stood and waved the bat. "I said don't move."

Nick looked at him in disgust and continued dressing. "What is it with you two and bats?"

Fully dressed, Nick dismissed Martin and turned an accusing glare to Jessie. "Now I understand why you said fucking me was 'fun.'"

"Wait a minute, you know him, Jessie? You *had sex* with him? How could—"

"What are you talking about, Nick?"

Nick's lips twisted. "It was all a big game to you."

"Nick, I don't know what's going on here. I was waiting for you and—"

"Really? And were you waiting for Martin, too?"

Jessie's confusion gave way to anger. How dare he accuse her of fucking both of them.

"My God, he knows my name! Jessie, how—"

"Martin, shut up. I can only deal with one idiot at a time." Jessie jumped out of bed and grabbed her robe.

"Answer the question, Jessie," said Nick.

She whirled toward Nick, her blood boiling. "I wasn't waiting for Martin. He was supposed to come over earlier."

She glared at Martin.

"Well. Thanks for answering the question. It's been . . . 'fun.'"

"Oh, for crying out loud," Jessie said, placing a hand on her forehead.

Nick turned and stalked out of the room. She heard him stomp down the stairs.

Seconds later, the front door slammed.

"Damn it," said Jessie, running a hand through her hair. She took a deep breath and turned to Martin. "What the hell are you doing here?"

"I came to get my stuff."

"Your 'stuff' is not in my bed."

"You invited me into your bed."

"I did not!"

"I asked if I could stay and you pressed your bottom against me then whispered, 'you came.'"

Oh. Right. But she'd thought he was Nick.

"Obviously, you were expecting someone else. I *thought* we should give us another chance, but . . ." He shook his head. "I don't think it's going to work, Jessie."

"I'm glad we finally agree, Martin."

He motioned towards the stairs with the bat. "Who was that, Jessie?"

"Oh, geez, enough, Martin."

She stalked forward, picked up his pants, shirt, and tie and thrust them into his free hand. She yanked the bat out of his other hand. "That is my new neighbor, whom I met the night that you failed to open the letter I sent to you by courier."

She ushered him out of the bedroom and down the stairs as she talked.

"Jessie, that's awfully fast. You're probably rebounding. I don't think—"

"Martin, I don't care what you think. We. Are. O-ver." They were at the front door. "I want my key and I will send you your stuff."

She waited for Martin to dress, then held out her hand for her key.

He sighed, dug into his pocket and took it off his key chain. He handed it to her. "Jessie—"

"Thank you and good-bye, Martin." She opened the front door, pushed him out, and shut the door behind him.

As she listened to him clatter down the front stairs, she leaned against the door. No sooner had she closed her eyes, than there was a knock on her door.

"For God's sake, Martin!" She yanked the door open. "Leave me—"

It wasn't Martin.

Her heart jangled in her chest. She forced herself to frown. "What are you doing here, Nick?"

"I came to let you explain."

"Don't do me any favors."

"I'd like to hear it."

"Well, I don't want to explain it."

Nick glared.

Jessie glared.

"What was Martin doing here?"

"He came to get his stuff."

"His stuff was in your bed?"

Their thought processes were in sync. If she'd been in a better frame of mind, she would've appreciated the irony. But fury didn't set the mood for humor. "He was supposed to come earlier. I'd assumed he'd forgotten. I was waiting for you, trying to stay up, but I drank a bottle of wine and got sleepy."

She crossed her arms. "Next thing I know, my room has been invaded by The Two Stooges."

Nick's lips twitched.

Jessie's lips tightened. "How could you have thought I'd sleep with Martin?"

He raised a brow. "Maybe when I caught him in bed with you?"

He had a point. "Well, why would I be stupid enough to invite Martin over the same night you were supposed to come by?"

"The question did occur to me."

She sighed in frustration. "Why didn't you let me explain?"

"I am now."

Oh. Right, again.

"Look, I overreacted. But, come on, Jessie. If the roles were reversed, wouldn't you have reacted the same?"

91

He had another point. God, she was beginning to hate being wrong. "No."

"No?"

"I would've yanked the covers back and ordered both of you out, then picked up your clothes and thrown them out the window, while calling both of you every name in the book, and telling you never to come back, then I would've called the police and obtained a restraining order . . ."

Jessie paused for breath.

Nick's mouth hung open.

Jessie smiled sweetly. "Sorry. Go on."

"Uh . . ."

She waited.

"Like I said, I wasn't thinking, rationally—that is. My mind instantly latched onto the belief that you'd just been having fun with me—in a bad away—that you'd been toying with me."

"Nick, I'm not . . . her."

"I know," he said softly. "That's why I like you."

Jessie remained silent, ignoring the flush of pleasure caused by his words, refusing to give into the pull of sweet-talk.

Nick grinned. "You have to admit, it was kind of funny."

Jessie's lips quirked. "Yeah . . . it was, I guess." Enough had been said. All was forgiven. "You want to come inside?"

"Yeah, under one condition."

Jessie frowned. "What condition?"

"That you promise to shave your hairy chest."

"Hairy—" Oh. Right. Martin's chest. He must've slipped his arms around Martin when he'd slid into bed.

Her laughter prevented her from finishing the sentence.

"Well? Will—"

Her kiss prevented *him* from finishing his sentence.

Sharice

A Sinful Phone Call

1

"Hi, Shawn. I'm the woman who was wearing the short red dress, standing on the corner—"

Damn.

Cringing at the words she'd just blurted, Sharice jabbed the pound key on the cell phone keypad to delete the voicemail message she'd just recorded. As the digital voice walked her through the instructions to rerecord her message, she stared out the windshield of her Lexus, idly noticing the after-eleven crowd in line in front of Club Maxwell's. Defying the chilly October air, the women wore their spaghetti-strap tops and tightest skirts, while standing proud in their three-inch strappy sandals.

She tried again.

"Hi, Shawn . . . This is Sharice. I met you outside of Maxwell's last Friday. I was talking to my friend when you shouted your number out the window . . ."

My God. Are the pickings for a night of sex so slim that I have to resort to this? Just hang up.

". . . and . . ."

Hang up.

"...well..."

Hang the fuck up.

But, damn, that man had been on her mind all week. It was once again Friday evening, and she somehow found herself cruising down the street in front of the club where they'd met. Her favorite song played on the radio—Jamie Foxx, crooning about how she needed a "G" like him to beat it, and Twista rapping about giving it to her in an elevator—and got her all hot and horny.

The same song had been playing softly from the depths of Shawn's Lex that night, too. Surely, that must be a sign. Just as the fact that his gleaming red car, identical to hers, was a sign. A sign that, unlike her last boyfriend, Darrell, and his 1990 Honda Civic, Shawn might actually treat her to dinner, instead of always crying broke. And Shawn's voice, as he'd practically begged her to call him, had sounded like liquid sex. That had been another sign.

The voice was a definite positive for a night of hot sex. For, if his technique was sad, she could just ask him to talk—and that sweet, slow, sexy tone would make up for any lack of finesse.

Sharice paused, about to delete her message again, when the song faded out on the radio and Tommy "Dr. Love" Jones came on.

"Now, that's a sinful song, isn't it?" He laughed. "It's definitely telling you to go out and sin, though not necessarily the way I'm advocating. I'm urging you, KPSX listeners, to go out and go for what you want, sin. Your happiness is just a sin away..."

Dr. Love was right. It was about time she "sinned." That is, do something she'd never done before. She turned her attention back to the phone.

"...Give me a holler at 510-555-1201," she finished.

Sharice clicked her phone off and tossed it onto the passenger seat, surprised to feel herself shaking from surplus adrenaline. How ridiculous that something as simple as calling a guy would spark the fight-or-flight response. On the other hand, maybe it wasn't so ridiculous, since she *never* called men first, period. She always waited for them to call her. Hell, she was no fool—she lived by the book *He's Just Not That Into You*, which was co-authored by Greg Behrendt.

Hence, she was committing a double sin—she was calling a guy first and she was calling a guy she hadn't even really met. And the only reason she'd broken her rule this time was because, well, it was kind of hard for a guy who didn't have her name or number to call her back.

So now what?

The line outside the club had grown another twelve feet since she'd arrived. Sharice did not do lines. Craning her neck forward, she looked to see if John was at the door. Yep. There he was, his bald, peanut-shaped head glistening in the soft light. He'd let her slide to the front of the line. There'd be no waiting tonight.

Sharice sighed. So what if she got in the club? Somewhere in between the time that she'd pulled out of her garage and pulled into this parking spot, Maxwell's had lost its appeal. The effort it would take to make meaningless small talk with a dozen or more men, in hopes of meeting one she wanted to take home for the night seemed like too much effort. Kind of like finding her contact lens in the Pacific Ocean.

She'd been feeling like this a lot lately, which is why she'd been celibate for months. *Six* months, to be exact.

A group of loud-talking sistahs—whose long hair did a better job of covering their asses than their skirts did—sauntered past the car. Did they really think people thought that horsehair was real?

Stop being so bitchy.

She should just go home. Her attitude was not male-magnet material.

But she didn't want to go home. Friday night was a prime party night, for crying out loud. And it was time for her to get her game back on track.

Sharice pressed the pad of her finger against the screen, turning up the radio. The deep voice of Dr. Love filled the car.

". . . Good luck, man . . . You're on, Jessie. What's your sin?"

Jessie giggled.

Sharice rolled her eyes.

"Well, a couple of months ago, I did a striptease for my boyfriend. It was something I'd always wanted to do, but had never done before . . ."

Dr. Love made a sound of approval.

Sharice snorted. "That ain't nothing. I've done a hundred stripteases."

". . . only it wasn't my boyfriend who saw it. It was my neighbor."

"Damn. I haven't done *that*," said Sharice.

Dr. Love laughed.

Jessie laughed. ". . . needless to say, the boyfriend's out and my neighbor is in."

"He's 'in'? Literally or figuratively?" asked Dr. Love.

Jessie and Dr. Love shared a chuckle.

Sharice joined in.

"Let's just say he's the new man in my life. Our relationship is wonderful. He—"

Sharice snorted. "I was feeling you until you ruined things with a 'relationship.' " She pressed the screen again, cutting Jessie off in mid-sentence; Sharice shook her head. A person had a better chance of winning the lottery than ending up in a relationship that worked. What was up with most women who were desperate for the big R? Sharice had tried that, twice, believing that she'd found *the one* each time. Instead, she'd discovered Malcolm had been living on the down low, sleeping with men behind her back. And Darrell had been sleeping with anything in a skirt, including whichever of her so-called friends he could get into bed—Sharice's bed.

Nope. She was through with that. Fool me once, shame on you; fool me twice, shame on me. Well, she was not going to be anyone's fool anymore. So now she just looked for a brotha for a good time.

But, for some reason, the "good times" were feeling fewer and farther in between. And Sharice's attitude was getting more and more frustrated. Not to mention her libido. She shrugged, throwing off her depressing thoughts.

Well, she might as well go inside the club. As she reached for her keys, her cell phone rang.

She glanced at the display on the cell phone. It was Shawn. Sharice grinned, no longer nervous now that she was back on familiar ground—being pursued.

She pressed a button to connect the call. "I like a guy who goes after what he wants."

"Uh . . ."

Damn, she was good. The throaty voice worked every time. "You *do* want something, don't you, Shawn?"

"Yeah . . . uh . . ."

She smiled. He was speechless, though the fact that he was surprised her a bit. From what little she'd been able to see of him in his car, the sly quirk of his lip—which passed for a smile—gave the impression that he was the type to have a snappy comeback.

"Well . . . ?" she prompted, converting the throatiness to a purr.

"Yes. Well. I'm not . . ."

He cleared his throat.

Sharice's smile widened.

"I'd like . . . you. Talk . . ."

She couldn't quite make out what he was saying, with the reception so bad. She'd only heard a few of the words and it sounded like he was far away, in a tunnel, with the wind blowing.

"What?"

". . . see you."

"You'd like to see me?" she repeated.

"Y . . ."

Was that a yes?

". . . now?" he asked.

"I can't hear you."

"Are you available now?"

She got it that time. He sounded like he was yelling, but his voice didn't register much louder. Where was he calling from?

Sharice paused. A woman should never appear too available, especially at 11:10 P.M. Even author Greg Behrendt would probably agree with that. She let her gaze drift back to Maxwell's, to the line that now looped around the corner. There'd be a good-size crowd inside. Odds were, even she could find someone interesting inside.

But she had someone who might be interesting right here, right now.

Screw Greg Behrendt. She didn't care if Shawn wasn't "into" her because she had no intention of being "into" him. After all, she wasn't looking for a relationship. She didn't have to go by all the rules.

"What do you have in mind?" she asked.

2

"Fuck!" Jamal slammed his fist against the steering wheel of his 1986 Toyota Camry as the engine continued to churn futilely. He didn't know if he was cursing because the car wouldn't start—yet again—or because he'd just messed up. Not only had he stuttered and stammered like a prepubescent idiot, he'd asked this Sharice to meet him at a bar. A bar four miles away from the freeway shoulder where he and his car were now stuck.

Why the hell hadn't he just told her he wasn't Shawn—that she'd called the wrong number, like the five women before her?

Because of that damn sexy voice, that's why. Unlike the women before her, he wanted to know why a woman who sounded that good would call a number some dog had shouted during a drive-by. He'd never heard a voice like Sharice's this side of 1-900-FANTASY. He grimaced at the memory, still unable to believe he'd sunk low enough to call a 900 number. Once.

Jamal turned the car off, pumped the gas pedal, and then turned the key in the ignition again. The churning was worse than before, giving no hint of turning over, making him think he'd flooded the engine—though, what did he know? Cars were not his game. Now, ask him whether Microsoft was out-performing Apple and he could quote figures that would make a stockbroker's mind spin.

Unfortunately, the figures that he was so passionate about made the mind of just about everyone else spin. Not in a good way.

Jamal yanked the keys from the ignition and picked up his cell phone to call a cab. It was dead. "Fuck!"

But all was not lost.

Forty-five minutes later, the cab he'd called from a pay phone after walking along the freeway to the nearest exit, pulled up in front of the Marriott Hotel to drop him off.

What were the odds that Sharice would still be waiting an hour later, even if she had received his message he'd left from the pay phone informing her that he was running late?

Jamal passed through the lobby and up the escalator to the second floor. The brightly lit bar, which catered more to business travelers than locals, was almost deserted except for a couple of suits talking around a table in the corner and the woman at the bar.

Her back was to him but what he could see was inspiring. The smooth caramel shoulders revealed by the black halter-top tied at her neck were kissable, the small waist molded by the tight material was grippable, and the round hips and even rounder ass atop the stool made him want to pull her off the stool and onto his lap. Damn. The things he could do with that. He let his gaze drift lower, to the shapely legs, crossed at the ankle, and the two-inch heeled sandals on her feet.

Daaaaamn.

The image of those legs wrapped around his waist flashed

through his mind, the tips of those sandals poking his ass as he thrust forward, pumping hard, gripping those hips—

His cock twitched.

He cursed, forcing his mind to focus on the mundane, like each step that he took to reach the bar. Like what he was going to say when he got there. He stopped at the vacant barstool next to her, inhaling a faint flowery scent wafting from skin that looked even more touchable, squeezable, kissable than it did twenty feet away.

She was fine, in a Beyoncé kind of way—which was not the kind of woman he dated. Ultra-fine women tended to be divas and divas tended to be high maintenance and materialistic, going for the showy brothas fronting in their Lexes and Jags. A serious, studious-looking man driving a dilapidated hoopdie didn't register in their consciousness—even if this type had a financial portfolio a hundred times more solid than their flashy counterparts. Or so he'd heard from both Byron and King, who dated only divas.

So what was he doing here?

Satisfying his curiosity. Saving a stranger from the clutches of a dog.

Yeah, right.

Jamal slid onto the stool. The woman gave no awareness of his presence, didn't say, *I'm sorry. I'm waiting for someone.* Which could mean that she'd given up on Shawn. Or that she wasn't Sharice.

"Hi, I'm . . ." *Shawn* ". . . Jamal. Are you—"

The question evaporated from his mind as she raised her head and turned to him, facing him head on. A slow burning fire seemed to simmer within her light brown eyes, as if she were on her back, under him, waiting for him to fill her, instead of in this near-empty room. Her glossy lips were parted, as if waiting for his lips to possess hers in a kiss that plundered and demanded.

His heart drummed.

His breath hung.

His cock surged.

For the first time in months, Jamal desired a woman more than a column of numbers on a performance statement.

Her shapely, succulent lips quirked in a smile. "No, I'm not."

Those three words throbbed with sexiness, curling around his cock, confirming that she was the woman he'd spoken to on the phone.

He raised a brow, happy to feel his eyebrows were still functional. "You're not . . .?"

"No, I'm not with anyone. No, I'm not married. No, I'm not expecting anyone . . ."

Jamal forced his mind from the hypnotic purr of her voice to her words. Alright, another question answered. She'd given up on Shawn. Smart woman.

Her tongue caressed her lower lip. ". . . well, I'm not expecting anyone *anymore*."

He gave himself a mental shake. Time to get his cool back on. "Maybe I wasn't going to ask any of those things."

"You were."

With forced casualness, he asked, "Why do you say that?"

The smile still curved her lips as she raised her glass, placed it against lips that he wanted to taste. He watched her throat ripple as she swallowed, suppressing the urge to lean forward and press his lips against her neck, tracing her throat with his tongue.

Suddenly, he was jealous of a glass of ice cubes.

"You stood in the doorway and stared at me, debating whether or not to come over and say something."

How had she seen him? His gaze left hers briefly, taking in

the mirrored surface covering the back of the bar, behind the hanging glasses. He hadn't noticed them before. Mystery solved. "Yeah, I did stare at you but that wasn't what I was debating."

She tipped her glass and inclined her head slightly. "Oh?"

No. I was watching the light on your skin, making it shine, making me want to run my tongue along a shoulder to see if you tasted salty or sweet or both, before I—

Forget that shit. Get to the point. Tell her you're not Shawn.

But maybe he didn't need to mention Shawn. After all, *she* didn't think he was Shawn.

"No. I knew I was going to come over to you. I was debating what to say when I got here."

"Honesty's a refreshing trait." She took another sip of her drink. Watching her the second time had the same effect it did the first time. Jamal licked his lips, wishing it was his cock—instead of the alcohol—entering her mouth, feeling the hot wetness caressing him, before moving to the back of her throat, feeling its tightness—

"Tell me, Jamal. Are you single?"

He blinked, returning his focus to the present. The glass was back on the black bar top, her fingertip circling the lip of the glass.

"Yes."

"Do you date a lot?"

"Enough."

Her laughter tickled his eardrums, causing a vibration to throb through his body and tighten the invisible hold she already had on his cock. It twitched again, harder this time.

"That's funny?" he asked.

"Your tone implies that you don't like dating."

"I don't." He forced a nonchalant shrug he was far from feeling. "The games. The posturing. It gets old real quick."

She nodded, though whether in agreement he couldn't tell. His gaze was drawn to her pink-tipped fingernail, tracing the rim of a tumbler.

"What are you drinking?" he asked.

"A Dirty Minnie."

"A Dirty Minnie? What's in that?"

"Stoli Strasberi, Vodka, Amaretto, Grenadine . . ." she shrugged ". . . and more."

Damn. "Strong stuff . . . May I buy you another one?"

"Thank you, but I've had enough."

Her finger kept circling the glass. The movement hypnotized, taking his mind back to the heels digging into his ass, and those fingertips gripping his shoulders to hold on before slipping to his back, squeezing and tracing his shoulders while her pussy squeezed and stroked his cock.

He interrupted the direction of his thoughts in disgust. What the fuck was wrong with him? He was acting like the dog he'd accused Shawn of being. He'd come here just to satisfy his curiosity.

His curiosity was satisfied.

He hadn't come here to pick her up, to take Shawn's place.

But he wanted to pick her up; he wanted to take Shawn's place. Despite the fact that he never picked up women in bars. Despite the fact that he steered clear of divas. Only, so far, he hadn't gotten the impression she was a diva. She didn't sound high-maintenance and demanding but . . .

How did he know what she was or was not? He knew nothing about her—though his cock was desperate to make her acquaintance.

That was another thing he never did: Let his cock lead the show—outside of the bedroom, that is. Jamal was always the epitome of control and reason, choosing women based on suitability criteria, of which sexual attraction was only one part—

"Have you ever stood a woman up?"

Ah, Shit.

"No." Enough. It was time to tell her. "Listen, I—"

"Would you stand *me* up, Jamal?"

The breathy sound of his name from her lips turned his mouth to cotton. Jamal swallowed hard, summoning moisture. "Uh, no. I—"

Her full, sexy lips quirked into a half-smile. "Right answer." The pink fingernail he'd watched trace the glass, moved to trace the same circles on his hand.

His cock jerked.

"Since you'd never stand me up, what would you like to do right now? With me?"

Her finger moved along his wrist, swirling along the sensitive skin, sending prickles up his arm and quivers through his cock.

Her voice said she knew exactly what he wanted.

Her skin moving against his skin, firing up his body and scaring all thoughts from his mind, told him what she wanted the answer to be.

He opened his mouth to give her his answer. The right answer.

3

Sharice watched Jamal's full lips part, as if he were going to say something, then close, as if he'd changed his mind. She stared into his brown eyes, keeping her gaze flirtatious and masking her anxiety. But she was operating on automatic pilot, going through the motions of being playful and sexy, while feeling anything but.

Unlike past appearances on the pick-up scene, she cared about the outcome to this one—cared if Jamal wasn't interested. Maybe because his chest didn't puff up—as if he'd just won the prize of the day, seeing her as a prize for his ego, instead of a woman with needs of her own—when she'd let him know she was attracted to him. Or maybe it was because he'd stared at her for a good few minutes before coming over to her, as if he were working up the courage to do so.

Though Lord only knew—with his maple-syrup eyes that had stolen her breath when she'd looked up at him; his sexy mouth that she'd like to trace with her finger before, during, and after she kissed him; and his shaved head that she'd love to run her hands over—why he'd felt the need to work up the courage. He surely got his share of female attention.

She moved her fingers higher, trailing over his forearm and up to his biceps. "Maybe you'd like to . . ."

She squeezed his biceps lightly, liking the firmness, liking the fact that he didn't just look muscular, he *was* muscular. She moved beyond his shoulder, trailing her fingertips inside his collar, caressing the chocolaty skin above it. Chocolaty skin that she was dying to taste, lick, suck.

". . . get to . . . know each other better?"

Jamal's eyes flared. "How much better?"

Sharice smiled, moving her fingers up his neck to his chin, flicking them along his lower lip. Softly tracing. Lightly touching. "Intimately better. Tonight, I want to get to know every inch of you. One night. No . . . complications."

Jamal's eyes darkened. "Are you sure you want that with *me*?"

Sharice licked her lower lip and dipped her finger inside Jamal's mouth. "Is there a reason why I shouldn't want that with you, Jamal?"

He moved his head back slightly so that Sharice's finger grazed his inner lip. His tongue appeared between his lips. He licked.

Sharice suppressed a gasp, a jolt of lust clenching her stomach at Jamal's sleepy gaze and liquid touch. He lifted his hand, wrapped his fingers around hers, and pulled her hand back. Brushing his lips across her knuckles, he produced another barely restrained shiver through her.

"Wait here," he said, giving her hand a squeeze before placing it back on the counter.

Watching him slide from the stool and walk to the exit, Sharice was pleased by the way his jeans hugged his ass.

God, what was she doing? She'd never before said just a

handful of words to a guy and then invited him to bed. The fun was making it long and leisurely. Like dancing close enough to feel the man's body heat caressing her skin, the occasional stroke of knee against thigh, the narrowed gaze stealing a hot glance down the "v" of her dress when he thought she wasn't looking, or watching her body move in sync with his as they danced, hips rotating and gyrating mere inches apart, mimicking private acts where hips and skin touched. The fun was in the teasing, in becoming so aroused that clothes were shed almost before the door of his place had closed, he was inside her before they made it to a bed, and it was over before it got started. The foreplay happened on the dance floor; the sex happened behind closed doors; and she could leave, satisfied. A passionate encounter that sparked immediately and was extinguished quickly. Since she was already aroused before sex, the guy didn't have to have a stellar technique to bring her to orgasm.

But she and Jamal had barely talked.

They'd barely touched.

There'd been no foreplay.

A tight body, sexy eyes, and a promising touch did not guarantee a satisfying sexual experience. While she felt aroused, she was a long way from pre-orgasmic. Which meant, depending on his technique, she might be stuck behind closed doors with him longer than usual. Which might lead to awkwardness. Awkwardness, like expectations of getting to know each other nonsexually.

So why had she propositioned him?

Jamal was back in front of her before she had the answer.

And she'd slipped her hand into his hand, slid off the stool, darted into the elevator, and was standing in front of a hotel room before she had a chance to change her mind.

As Jamal opened the door and led her into the room, her mouth dropped open.

He'd rented a suite.

To the right was a sitting area with a plush couch and matching chair. Behind that was a dining area, with a tall circular table and tall black chairs. A bar and a kitchenette with black granite countertops rounded out the room.

Unease skittered up her back. A suite seemed a bit too elaborate for a one-night stand. Sharice looked beyond Jamal's shoulder, caught a glimpse of where he was leading her, and tugged his hand, stopping him.

He turned back, his brow lifted in inquiry.

Sharice sidled up to him, smiling seductively—or so she hoped, for she suddenly felt nervous. She didn't want him to lead her to the bedroom. She wanted to get the party started here, in the living room, now. Preferably, against a wall or across the couch.

Somehow, the bedroom seemed too intimate.

Pressing herself against him, she slid her hands up his back, to his neck, to the back of his head, where she pulled him to her, lowering his head. His lips touched hers, soft and firm at the same time. Soft in feel, but firm in what they wanted—to taste, to explore.

He took control of the kiss, ending her teasing nibbles, parting her lips and thrusting inside. His hand cupped her head, guiding her to where he wanted her to be, controlling the pressure.

His tongue met hers, then retreated.

Her tongue explored his, then retreated.

Advancing and withdrawing, lips and mouths fought for dominance.

Sharice moved her hand restlessly over his back, sliding under the cotton shirt to feel flesh. Smooth, muscular flesh.

A gasp escaped her. Jamal swallowed it, his lips pressing harder against hers, his tongue probing deeper, demanding more.

She moved her hips against his, feeling his cock jerk against her pelvis.

A thrill of power thrummed through her, stoking the lust that was welling up inside her. He was hot. She was hot. This was about sex.

To prove the point, Sharice moved her hands along his waist, dipping under the waistband of his jeans.

His skin quivered.

She slid her hands to the front, fumbling for the button, unsnapping, unzipping.

Jamal inhaled sharply before moving her hands away. He drew away.

Sharice opened her dazed eyes and looked into his. "Change your mind?" Her tone was supposed to be teasing. It echoed with traces of pleading instead.

He smiled. A sexy, heavy-lidded smile that told her his mind was in sync with his cock.

She pulled him toward her again.

He pulled away, stepping back.

"I want to take a shower."

Sharice blinked, her mind attempting to focus on his words. She couldn't remember the last time a guy had pulled away to go shower—well, maybe after a hot workout session on the couch or floor or both of the above. She resisted the urge to turn her head and do a quick smell test.

"Okay," she lied. It wasn't okay. She didn't want to stop.

Still wearing the smile, Jamal turned, keeping hold of her hands and pulling her along behind him into the bathroom.

Oh. He meant he wanted them to take a shower *together*.

A frisson of discomfort bubbled in her stomach. She hadn't taken a shower with a man since Darrell. There'd been candles and champagne, which they hadn't touched until afterward, so anxious they'd been to fuck.

Only, it hadn't been just a fuck—or so she'd thought, until she'd walked in on the same scene with him and her best friend weeks later. It didn't take a doctorate degree to know that he just wasn't that "into" her.

She stopped in front of the sink, causing Jamal to turn back to her.

She tried to remove her hand from his grasp.

He held tight.

"You go ahead. I'll shower after you," she said.

"Hmmm." Jamal released her hands, sliding them up her arms, his gaze following their action, as if there was something interesting to their movement. Trailing her shoulders, they circled inward, tracing the neckline of her top, to the hint of cleavage.

Her skin prickled under his path.

Her breath hitched, though whether from the touch of his fingers or the intense way he stared at her body as if memorizing every line, she didn't know.

His fingertip dipped into the valley between her breasts, before moving down. Both hands rested on her waist.

"You want to take a shower alone?" he asked, his hands lightly stroking her waist.

No. "Yeah."

He stared at her, his dark eyes taking in her eyes, before moving to her lips, lingering. When his gaze returned to hers, his eyes resembled melted Belgian chocolate.

Hot. Wet. Gooey.

"Okay," he said, sliding his hands under the hem of her dress, over the outside of her thighs and hips, and up the sides of her body.

Sharice shivered, unable to stop herself.

"Lift your arms."

"What are you doing?"

114

"Getting you ready for your shower."

Sharice laughed, suddenly self-conscious. It was one thing to undress while caught up in the moment, but . . . under the harsh fluorescent lighting while in the midst of a nonsexual conversation, well, that felt . . .

"Shy?"

Sharice laughed again. "No." And it was true. She didn't have a shy bone where her body was concerned. No, Jamal made her feel off-balance. Things were happening that shouldn't be happening. Fast and furious sex wasn't happening like it was supposed to. Shit, forget about fast and furious sex—*nothing* was happening yet.

If nothing is happening, why are you tripping?

Jamal tugged on her shirt. "Up."

Sharice shrugged off the question and lifted her arms.

Her dress came off.

Her bra sprung apart as Jamal unhooked it.

He paused, his gaze roving her breasts. "Beautiful," he whispered, skimming a fingertip over the swell of her breast before lowering his head.

Sharice held her breath.

His lips grazed the top of her breasts, kissing lightly, softly, before he withdrew.

Nooooooo . . .

Sharice suppressed a groan, forcing herself to remain still, not giving in to the urge to grab his head and guide it to the nipples that had hardened, despite the fact that he hadn't touched them. Nipples that strained for his touch and tongue, despite that fact that he had neither stroked nor licked them.

Jamal drew back, his hands dropping to her waist, slipping under the waistband of her panties, before drawing them down over her hips. They fell silently to the floor.

Jamal stood silently, staring. His hands rested on either side of her lower hips. "Beautiful," he said again, his voice barely above a strained whisper. His hands moved inward.

Sharice gasped.

His thumbs lightly caressed the lips that pulsed with need, beating and throbbing, as if her heart had suddenly landed there.

She tilted her hips upward, guiding his fingers to where she wanted them, begging him with her body to separate her pussy lips, and stroke her lightly, then slightly harder. Slow, then faster.

Instead, Jamal moved his hands over her hips and took a step back. "Since you want to shower alone, you can watch me."

With one smooth movement, his polo shirt was over his head and on the floor.

Sharice watched muscled biceps and toned abs with lustful eyes.

In a second smooth movement, the button on his jeans was undone, his zipper was unzipped, and briefs and jeans slid over lean hips.

Sharice watched the muscles in his thighs clench as he stepped out of the circle of his clothes, watched his cock jerk upward, straining toward her, as he straightened again. "If you'd like to join me at any time . . ."

With a half-smile, he turned, threw the shower curtain back and leaned over the faucet.

Sharice leaned back against the sink, feeling weak-kneed at the sight of two perfectly toned ass cheeks. God, did this man have an ounce of flab anywhere on his body? The jeans and baggy shirt had hinted at muscles but . . . damn. Most guys with a body like Jamal's would be flaunting it, not hiding it behind loose clothing.

Water gushed out of the showerhead. Jamal tore open the

package of soap, grabbed a wash cloth, and stepped into the tub. Leaving the curtain open, he turned to face her and lathered up the wash cloth, then moved away from the spray of water.

His hand brushed an arm, shoulder, and chest, before repeating the action on the other side.

White soapy foam bubbled on his mocha skin.

Sharice swallowed hard, summoning moisture for her parched throat.

Jamal reached behind him, soaping up his back.

Sharice resisted the urge to do it for him.

His hands returned to the front, running over his chest and abs and hips and—

Sharice groaned.

—Cock.

The cloth hid his cock for a second, before he tossed it aside. His hands stroked it. "It would be a shame to waste this." His voice was husky.

Yes, it would be a damn shame.

Jamal's hand pumped, sliding over and around the head of his penis, then back down.

Sharice's heart pumped, pushing the blood through her, pooling it between her legs, where her pussy still throbbed and pulsed in sync with her heart.

It's time to sin. Dr. Love's words rang through her head.

He was right. She'd been sinning ever since she took the initiative and called Shawn. Why stop now? Why should she fight the delectable specimen in front of her, flexing muscles she couldn't wait to touch, stroking a cock she couldn't wait to feel inside her?

She didn't want to stop. Didn't want to worry about the past or the future. No sense in letting it ruin what appeared to be a perfectly good shower fuck.

Is that all that's going on here, a shower fuck?

Sharice ignored the question and pushed away from the sink. She walked toward the shower and stepped inside. She let her gaze run the length of Jamal as her hand circled his cock.

He jerked in her hand. The breath exploded from his lips, bouncing off of her neck.

Sharice pumped her hand, loving his smooth hardness. Her heart raced. Her breath shook. "No, I definitely do not want this to go to waste." Her voice was shaky.

With one hand on her shoulder, he guided her under the flow of the water. With the other, he wrapped his hand around hers and stopped her ministrations to his cock.

"You don't like that?" she asked.

"I love that. But first things first." He reached back, grabbed a clean cloth from the rack and lathered it with soap. His hands glided over her neck and shoulders, down the front of her arms and up the backside, to her side, across her stomach, to the undersides of her breasts.

There was nothing overtly sexual about the touch, but Sharice's nerve endings sparked with arousal.

There was nothing about the cloth rubbing along her skin that should have made her feel tense, but she did. The fact that Jamal watched the progress of the white cotton caressing her skin, coupled with the palms of his hands that followed, smoothing the soap bubbles along her flesh, as if he had all the time in the world, as if this was enough for him, as if this was not leading to the fuck that she imagined.

That was what made her uncomfortable.

His actions were intentional. As if he knew her need to hurry but wanted to keep it slow, drawing it out, making it last longer than it should.

Sharice wanted to move, to reach out and squeeze the cock

that still reached for her, that still beckoned to her hand, to spur him on.

But she didn't.

Instead, she stood still, marveling at the sense of vulnerability that she thought she'd long ago lost, awestruck by Jamal's enjoyment of her body in a way she couldn't remember anyone enjoying her body ever. Not Malcolm. Not Darrell. Not any of the casual sex partners after them.

Jamal's touch and his intense gaze combined to make what should feel like a fuck, feel like making love, thereby turning what she thought was making love with Malcolm and Darrell into fucks.

They hadn't treated her body with this reverence, this admiration. They hadn't treated her body with love.

But Jamal was.

Her head spun with the realization.

Jamal's hands, spreading soap over her breasts, sent her head spinning for an entirely different reason.

She gasped.

He smiled, moving his hand down her ribcage and over her abdomen, stopping at the bottom, where her stomach gave way to pelvis, and pelvis led to pussy, which lead to—

Sharice pressed into his hand.

Jamal moved his hand to her hip, holding her still, while using the other one to drag the washcloth over her hips, to her ass, then back to her thighs.

"I didn't know you were sadistic," she said, her voice trembly.

"I'm not."

"Oh? Then this slow torture is supposed to be pleasurable?"

He smeared soap over her thighs, his fingertips grazing her swollen lips.

"It would be . . ." His finger dipped inside.

Sharice stumbled.

". . . If you let yourself feel it."

Oh, she was going to feel it all right. His finger was where she wanted it. Finally.

"Are you going to feel it?"

"Yes."

"Good. Because I want you to feel it. I want you to feel me."

One second, he was standing and the next he was kneeling before her, his gaze riveted to the spot where his finger explored. Moving his hand higher, he used his fingers to pull her pussy lips up and apart. He leaned forward. His lips touched her pussy in a light kiss. His tongue dipped between her lips, giving her one . . . long . . . lick.

Oh. God.

"Like that?" he asked, his breath heating her already inflamed pussy.

"Yessss."

"I like it, too." He lapped again. And again. And again.

Sharice fell back against the wall, letting her head loll back and her eyes half close. Her nails raked the slick tiled wall of the shower, grasping for purchase that was not there. The water poured from the spigot, pounding in her ears, hitting her shoulders and side, bouncing off of her body, off the walls, and off the tub.

Jamal's tongue stroked.

Sharice's legs trembled. Fire pooled in her stomach, spilling over, spreading out, climbing higher.

Jamal gripped her hips, both guiding her and supporting her, as his tongue drove her higher, leaving her breathless, panting, wanting, needing.

Sharice held his head, which felt smooth and wet, using her hands to ask for more pressure, first guiding, then caressing.

He got it. His laps were faster and harder, longer and deeper.

She tried to hang on to the feeling, to suppress the crescendo of sensation, to make it last.

But she couldn't. Jamal wouldn't let her. Sharice let out a cry when orgasm burst from her hold.

Sensation slammed through her.

She moaned.

Her legs buckled.

Dropping her hands to his shoulders, she gripped the hard muscle to keep herself upright.

Jamal's licks became soft kisses, no longer caressing her sensitive clit, instead caressing her outer lips.

As the last shudder faded from her body, she became aware of the water beating on her, beating on Jamal, beading on his smooth skull and his buff shoulders before rolling off.

Awe replaced arousal.

Shock replaced sensation.

While she enjoyed oral sex, Sharice had never orgasmed from it. Oh, she'd pretended to, when the guy she was with tried real hard. But she'd rarely been able to let go, namely because the guys she'd let do it seemed to do it because it was expected, not because they seemed to enjoy it. They gave her clit and pussy about twenty seconds of attention, before whipping out their cocks and plunging in.

Which was fine with her, since she managed to come anyway.

But Jamal hadn't stopped.

Jamal hadn't come yet.

Jamal hadn't seemed to kiss and lick her because it was expected. In fact, it was the opposite. She hadn't asked for it. Jamal seemed to have done it because he'd wanted to. Because he desired her—and wanted her to desire it, too.

And she had let go. She hadn't had to force unwanted

thoughts from her mind. She didn't have any thoughts in her mind. Just feeling. Just sensation. Just pleasure.

And she'd come. Why?

She didn't want to think about why he'd been the first to make her come this way. She didn't want to think about why not once had she thought about this as a fuck.

She didn't want to think about why—

Jamal rose, placed his hands on her shoulders and turned her toward the wall. The wet tile chilled her cheek. His chest pressed against her back. His cock jerked against her ass. "My God. I can't believe how beautiful you are."

His hands dropped to her hips, gripping.

His breath hit her neck, heating.

His teeth nipped her shoulder, biting.

Jamal grabbed her hands, holding them above her head against the tile, while rubbing his hips against her ass, his cock probing the entrance to her pussy. "Is this what you want?" he demanded.

The arousal that had been replaced by awe zoomed through her again.

The sensation that had been replaced by shock jolted her.

This she was familiar with. This she could handle. "Yes, that's what I want."

He ran his lips over her shoulder, stopping at the sensitive spot no one before had ever discovered. He licked hard. He sucked hard. Heat sparked her pussy.

"What do you want?" he rasped.

"I want—"

His cock entered her pussy, pausing after only the head was covered.

Sharice moaned. "I want you to fuck me."

Jamal laughed. "Yeah, I know—that's what you *think* you want."

His cock slid into her another inch.

Sharice gasped.

"But *I* think you want . . ."

And another inch.

Sharice jutted her hips back.

". . . This." Jamal caught her mouth with his and slowly pressed his hips forward at the same time.

His cock filled her pussy.

His tongue filled her mouth.

Sharice moaned.

Jamal swallowed her moan. His tongue slowly circled—grazing her teeth, the roof of her mouth, before suckling her tongue. Exploring thoroughly, moving purposely, as if savoring every taste, memorizing every crevice.

She craned her neck further back, seeking to taste more of him.

She pressed her hips back, attempting to feel more of him.

Jamal moved away, withdrawing his cock, then moved forward, burying his cock. His hands released hers and gripped her hips, holding her still, forcing her to endure this excruciatingly slow pace.

He broke his mouth from hers, trailing his tongue along her cheek, to her earlobe.

He nipped.

She shivered.

"This . . ." he whispered, dotting her jaw with feathery kisses. He moved his hips back, leaving only the tip of his cock inside.

". . . is what . . ."

He licked her neck lightly and moved his hips forward, inching into her slowly.

". . . you want . . ."

He kissed her neck tenderly and ground his hips against her ass, rotating one direction, then the other.

"Isn't it?" he breathed into her ear.

Desire that Sharice thought he'd satisfied with his tongue, flared from his cock.

His hands slid from her hips, over her ass, and between her legs to her lips, spreading them, zeroing in on her clit.

He rubbed.

She climbed.

His hips remained unmoving, locked in place, pressing her flat against the tile. Sharice was imprisoned between the wall and him, unable to move, forced to remain motionless.

He jerked his cock rhythmically inside her pussy, the sensation magnified by his still body.

She clenched her muscles, holding him tight inside her.

"Tell me this is what you want. My touch. My desire. My kiss. All of me."

He twitched.

She gripped.

His fingertips danced along her flesh, making her dizzy, making her breathless, making her aware of nothing but him. His body . . . his fingers . . .

"Tell me."

. . . his words.

But she couldn't tell him in words. Instead, her body quaked, her legs trembled, and heat once again exploded inside her, speeding her heart, consuming her breath, and forcing a cry from her throat.

The seconds ticked by in silence. She couldn't speak. Wouldn't speak.

Finally, the room came back into focus. Sharice became aware of the heat from Jamal's body, tense and rigid against hers; the hardness of his cock still resting inside her, while the cold seeped into her breasts, stomach, and thighs from the wet tiles she was pressed against. The water hitting her had also gone from comfortable heat to barely lukewarm.

Sharice shivered.

"You couldn't even bring yourself to say it, could you?" His voice was soft.

His words hurt her ears.

"You wanted this . . ." His cock, still hard, jerked inside her. ". . . and you wanted me . . ." His mouth moved over hers, softly, gently, tenderly, as if her lips were fragile.

She couldn't kiss him back.

"Why can't you admit it?"

It was fitting that the water suddenly turned from lukewarm to cold. It matched her insides for she felt cold—frigid, even— inside. She couldn't admit it because . . . she'd felt empty for so long. She'd become comfortable with that emptiness because she didn't have to feel, didn't have to want, didn't have to hurt. Jamal was asking her to let go of that emptiness, to let him in. And the thought of doing that turned her insides to ice.

Jamal kissed her cheek lightly and withdrew from her, then moved away. She heard him turn the water off and pull open the shower curtain. She turned away from the wall, just in time to see his outstretched hand with the towel.

"Thank you," she said, taking it with a small smile but not looking at him.

Awkwardness had set in. She felt awkward because something had happened that wasn't supposed to happen. Whether or not she wanted to admit it, Jamal was right. She had wanted more. For once, she wasn't just feeling body parts licking, kissing, and entering her. Despite being caught up in the sensations he'd caused to swirl within her, she'd been aware of the man attached to the sensations. She'd felt a connection to him.

Sharice did not do "connections."

She toweled dry hurriedly, then stepped out of the shower, and reached down to pick up her clothes.

Jamal grabbed her hand, which brought her eyes to his. "Stay," he said.

"I can't."

Because if she did, she might want to stay longer. Then she'd want to see him again. And before she knew it, she'd be calling in to *The Sin Club* telling Dr. Love that she wanted a relationship. But, unlike Jessie, her foray into the relationship arena would not end happily.

It never did.

"You can't stay—or you won't?"

Sharice's attention turned back to Jamal. "Can't" implied that there was something preventing her from staying, while "won't" implied free choice, a mere decision not to do something.

Sharice's sense of panic around staying did not feel like free will.

"I can't."

Jamal's hand drifted up her arm, stroking and persuading. "What are you afraid of?"

"I'm not afraid of anything." *Liar.* "Look, it was great—you were great—but I don't do the strings thing."

"I'm not asking you for 'strings.' I'm just asking you to stay the night. Sleep with me in a bed. Let me make love to you in a bed."

Make love. The words sent an unwanted rush of pleasure through her veins while simultaneously causing her stomach to turn. She gently removed her grasp from his. "I'm sorry, Jamal. And I'm sorry that you didn't get to . . ." *come* ". . . finish . . . I feel really bad about that—"

"Then stay."

"I have to go." She stretched forward and brushed a kiss

against his lips. His unmoving lips. She walked away from him and quickly dressed.

Still not looking at him, she picked up her purse.

"Thanks," she said lamely and walked out the door.

Jamal stared at the door, resisting the urge to smash his hand against it. What the fuck had just happened? Minutes ago, he'd been holding the most delectable ass, his body rubbing against the softest skin he could remember feeling, drugged by the scent of soap and woman and need, his cock harder than he could remember, her pussy gripping him so tightly he'd wanted to pump into her forever.

And he hadn't been the only one into it. He'd felt her body vibrate with desire, shudder when he'd made her come with his mouth. And he'd felt her spasm around him when he'd been inside her, which had sent his need spiraling upward, his come spiraling outward—

Your come didn't spiral outward.

Shit.

He reached down to pick up his briefs from the floor, then paused. His briefs would have to wait a minute, wait until he erased all thought of Sharice's wild response to his body, his touch, his tongue—

Damn, she had tasted good. Like—

His cock surged.

He yanked his briefs over his hips, glad for the discomfort, the perfect punishment for standing here, mooning over some woman who obviously didn't want him.

And why didn't she want him? Because, instead of giving her the fuck she'd wanted, he'd said all that wimpy shit about what *he* wanted her to want. He'd done shit that left him feeling weak, shit that women supposedly wanted—like, want men to want them, need them, take care of them. That's what he'd tried to do for Sharice. But it'd been the wrong approach with the wrong woman.

Maybe if he'd been the smooth "playa" type he suspected Shawn of being, she'd still be with him right now—in bed, making that come-inspiring sound in the back of her throat, panting and writhing with need under him, while he held himself off of her, staring into her heavy eyes, taking in her parted lips, as he thrust inside her, watching her eyes lose focus as the turmoil he was causing in her body forced her to notice only what her body was feeling, what he was making her feel, what—

His cock, which had been starting to go down, returned to its granite state.

Jamal yanked his jeans from the floor and put them on.

Well, he wasn't Shawn. Though, for one split second, he wished he was. Because Shawn wouldn't have demanded more than she wanted to give. Wouldn't have wanted more than she wanted. Wouldn't have made her feel trapped, because the last thing a playa wants is a trap.

And, most importantly, Shawn wouldn't be standing here thinking about her after she'd walked out the door.

4

A couple hours later, Sharice sat in her car, staring out over Lake Merritt with her cell phone in her hand. Since leaving Jamal, she'd driven around aimlessly, not wanting to go home. What would she do there? She wasn't sleepy and she was too restless to watch a movie or read a book. She didn't even feel like clubbing—something that seemed to be happening more and more frequently.

So, she'd driven South on I-880 for over an hour, then turned around and headed back home to Oakland. Instead of going to her apartment, she'd stopped at the lake. All the while, she'd been thinking—thinking about how to get rid of the panic Jamal had inspired. The last few years, she'd been happy being footloose and fancy-free. Not once had she wished for a connection with some brotha.

Until tonight.

Why? Just because he'd made her come in a way no man had before?

No.

The connection had started before that, had started down in the bar, when he'd approached her. He'd almost seemed vulnerable—not like the practiced men she was used to meeting. She'd been drawn to him, despite the fact that he hadn't issued one smooth line, made one empty compliment.

Which was a big reason for the attraction. Which was a big reason for her discomfort. Because, somehow, he seemed to see beneath the surface to the things she wanted to hide. Which made her feel . . . vulnerable.

Well, you know what to do when you feel vulnerable.

Run away from things, that's what.

"I am not running away."

Yes, you are.

Sharice frowned. No, she wasn't. She just knew what she didn't want. She didn't want a connection, which could lead to the desire for a relationship, which would lead to heartbreak.

Been there, done that.

Maybe Jamal is different.

Sharice snorted and flipped open her cell phone. Yeah, right. Enough of this thinking. The only way to get rid of these thoughts was to get back on track, to go for the one-night kind of man she'd been looking for. Well, not tonight. Jamal had left her more than satisfied. No, now she'd just set something up for . . . soon.

To wipe away the memory of Jamal.

She dialed the number that had started this whole mess with Jamal, holding little hope that it'd be answered at 3:47 A.M. While the phone rang, she stared at the light from the streetlights reflecting off the water.

Shawn answered on the second ring, taking her by surprise.

"Oh. Hi, Shawn, this is Sharice."

A slight pause. "Hi, Sharice."

His voice sounded . . . funny. Deeper and huskier than last time. Of course, the last time, the connection had been so bad, she could barely hear him. Now he sounded clear.

She said, "Did I call at a bad time?"

"I got a minute."

"I got that message you left earlier, but there was a lot of static so I couldn't make it out. Were you calling to make it up to me for standing me up?"

"Then, I was calling to tell you I had car problems. Now, I'm . . ." He paused then continued, ". . . offering to make it up."

"Oh? And what are you going to do to make it up to me?" she asked, forcing a teasing playfulness to her tone.

Another pause, then, "I'm going to give you what you wanted when you . . . called me."

"A drink, Shawn?" she asked with mock innocence, injecting a purr to her voice she didn't really feel.

What was wrong with her? Why did she feel . . . empty, like she was watching herself go through the motions from a distance, without really feeling anything?

He laughed, his laugh reminding her of Jamal's.

She suppressed a snort of disgust. She was *not going* to think of Jamal. She *was going* to get into this with Shawn.

"Where are you?" he asked, changing the subject.

Parked at Lake Merritt, trying not to think. "In my car."

"What are you doing now?"

Trying to forget about Jamal. "Sitting here, talking to you."

"What are you wearing?" Shawn's voice took on a raspy sound.

Sharice's laugh sounded forced to her own ears. "This is starting to sound like phone sex."

"It is." The huskiness in his voice reminded her of Jamal. The way Jamal had sounded when he'd slipped his finger into her pussy and told her it'd feel good if she let it.

And it had felt *sooooo* good as he'd dipped and swirled, rubbed and stroked—

A flash of arousal zipped through her—the first one she'd felt since she'd made the phone call.

Phone sex.

Right. She could do that. She'd never done it before, but she could do it. Replace thoughts of Jamal with thoughts of . . . what was his name? The guy on the phone?

Shawn.

Right. Shawn. What had he asked her? Oh yeah, what was she wearing. "Okay. I'm wearing—"

"Black."

"How'd you know that?"

"Because black is my favorite color."

Sharice's laugh felt a little more natural. "Okay. What are you wearing?"

"Jeans."

Jamal had been wearing jeans.

"Button fly or zipper?"

"Zipper." Like Jamal's.

Oh, for God's sake, 99 percent of men have jeans with zippers.

To get herself and the conversation back on track, she said, "If I asked you to unzip your jeans right now, would you?"

"Yes."

"Okay. Do it."

"Okay . . . I did it."

Like Jamal had done it—unzipped his jeans, hooked his fingers underneath the waistband of the denim and his briefs, the movement of his hands taking her breath with the material as his flesh was bared before her eyes. Mouthwatering thighs, fantasy-inducing cock . . .

"Are you hard?" she asked.

"Do you want me to be?"

"Yes . . ."

Jamal had been hard before he'd even touched himself, had been rigid with need by the time she'd wrapped her hands around him. And yet, he'd taken his time, seemingly having no desire to rush.

"Okay . . . I imagined you touching me. I'm hard." Shawn's voice sounded strained.

Like Jamal's had been when he'd asked her to stay, to make love with him in the bed.

"Good. Because I am touching you, . . ." *Jamal* ". . . Shawn. I'm running my fingertips down the length of your cock, over the head, then skimming the underside, before taking you in my hand . . ."

Sharice saw herself with Jamal—as she would have been if she hadn't left. Jamal in the bed in the hotel room. She would be naked. He would be naked. She would push him back into the pillows, his dark head adding beautiful color to the white linen. She would straddle him, his cock resting between the folds of her pussy, pressing up against her clit. She would move her hips against his, creating friction that would send delicious tingles radiating from where their flesh touched. Her movements would become frenzied, demanding, needing the release that hovered . . . right . . . in . . . her—

". . . and . . . ?" prompted Shawn, bringing her attention back to him.

She told Shawn that she pumped his cock with her hand, loving the way it felt, imagining how it would feel inside her, filling her.

But her mind pictured Jamal's cock, returned to the image of Jamal beneath her, of an orgasm rocking her as she rocked against him. She imagined crying out his name, seconds before their positions were switched and she was underneath him.

Shawn whispered her name, causing Jamal's image to evaporate.

Heavy breathing echoed over the phone seconds before she heard Shawn's muttered curse.

His release caressed her eardrums.

Her tension grew, her own release trapped within, wanting to come out. But not with Shawn. *Oh, Jamal,* she thought, imagining his lips—

"What did you say?" Shawn demanded.

"What?" Sharice asked, disoriented.

"You said something. It sounded like a guy's name."

Fuck. Had she really said Jamal's name out loud? She was really losing it. Quickly, she said, "No, I just moaned. Uh, I probably ought to hang up . . ."

Seconds ticked by.

Finally, he asked, "Wanna come by?"

"No. It's late."

Shawn laughed. "Baby, for what you started, it's still early."

"Well, I've got an early morning today," she lied.

"Aw'ight. Tomorrow, then?"

A booty call in the offering. Wasn't that what she'd called to set up?

"Let's see how we feel later, okay?"

"Cool. Keep in touch."

He sounded relieved that she didn't want to get together. Or maybe it was happiness she heard?

Sharice shrugged. She didn't care. Whatever it was, she was glad he hadn't pressed the issue. They'd both gotten what they wanted, right? He'd gotten off and she'd gotten . . . gotten . . .

To fantasize about Jamal, about what might have happened if she hadn't left. If she'd had the courage to admit the truth—that she *had* wanted his touch, his desire, his kiss.

All of him.

She started the car, backed out of the parking space, and squealed onto the road. She had somewhere to be.

She only hoped she wasn't too late.

5

Sharice rapped her knuckles against the hotel suite door and waited, listening for the sound of footsteps on the other side.

She heard nothing.

What if Jamal had already gone, left the room despite the fact that he'd paid for the night? She didn't have his phone number. Didn't have his last name. Nor did he have her last name—hell, had she even told him her first name? Anyway, there was no way for them to contact each other.

Sharice chewed her lower lip and raised her hand to knock again. Before her fingers touched the wood, the door opened.

Jamal, shirtless, stood in the doorway.

"Hey," she said, forcing a light smile.

"Hey," said Jamal, unsmiling. His expression neither encouraged nor discouraged.

Sharice kept her eyes on his face, trying not to notice the muscular chest sparsely covered with curly hair, until the eye moved downward to the darker dusting of curlicues peeking above the unbuttoned jeans.

Damn, she wanted him. She wanted to touch him and hold him and press herself against his tight body.

But the indifference that seemed to radiate from him didn't invite that now.

"I didn't think you'd be here," she said.

He raised a brow. "So that's why you came back? Because you didn't think I'd be here?"

"Well, I'd . . . *hoped* you'd be here because . . ." Sharice shrugged, trying to make something serious seem nonchalant. ". . . you were right."

"Right? About what?"

"Right about the fact that . . ." She shrugged again. ". . . that . . . *that* was what I wanted."

She held her breath, hoping that he wouldn't make her explain what she meant by "that." Prayed that he wouldn't make her say the words she hadn't been able to say earlier.

He stared at her, his eyes dark and unreadable.

She licked her lips. "I want to . . ." *make love* ". . . sleep with you. In the bed."

Her heart thundered against her ribcage.

Her palms felt clammy.

Her face felt warm.

Damn, this is hard.

And still Jamal remained silent.

"Are you going to let me in or do you want me to go?" The indifference in her voice pleased her.

Time seemed to crawl as she and Jamal stood frozen on opposite sides of the door. Finally, Jamal stepped to the side.

Relief whooshed out of her as she entered the room.

After closing the door, Jamal walked through the living room. She followed him, ending up in the bedroom. Stopping at the bed, he unzipped his jeans and slid them down over his lean hips. This time, he wasn't wearing any underwear. His cock was ready to perform.

Damn. Did he stay in a constant state of readiness?

Okay. It looked like they were not going to waste time talking. Which worked for Sharice, since she couldn't believe that she was back here and didn't want to think anymore about what this could mean.

Though her heart jangled in her chest, she smiled. She drew the dress up over her head, then quickly stripped off her bra and panties, making no attempt to make her actions sexy.

Jamal's eyes had changed from brown to black as they slowly traveled down her body and back up. His nostrils flared and a vein throbbed noticeably in his cock, visible from ten feet away.

Obviously, an erotic striptease wasn't a necessary aphrodisiac for him.

Though his gaze never left hers, Jamal reached down and threw the covers back on the bed, then straightened.

Waiting.

Sharice walked forward and climbed into bed, lying on her back. She smiled up at Jamal and stretched sinuously.

She waited.

Jamal slid into bed beside her, then turned her onto her side and pressed his body against her back. She gasped as she felt his hand reach between their bodies and grasp his cock, positioning it, moving it—

Sharice frowned and pressed her butt backward against him. Where she had previously felt his cock, she felt nothing.

He'd tucked it between his legs.

She turned back to face him. "What are you doing?"

"Giving you what you asked for."

Her frown deepened. "What?"

Jamal's eyes were serious but something seemed off. "You said you wanted to *sleep* with me."

Sharice flopped back onto her back and punched Jamal lightly on the arm.

This time, there was no mistaking his expression. He was smiling.

"You know that I meant—"

She didn't have a chance to finish the sentence, for Jamal leaned forward and captured her mouth with his. His lips moved softly over hers, giving her a kiss meant to stoke passion slowly, to fuel her desire lightly.

He drew back.

Sharice opened her eyes, staring up into eyes that appeared to regard her seriously—for real this time.

"Why'd you come back?" he asked.

Oh, shit. So much for not talking.

She raised her hand to Jamal's chest and trailed her finger between his pecs. "Because after . . ." *phone sex with Shawn . . .* Sharice suppressed a flash of guilt. Not that she had any logical reason to feel guilty. She didn't owe Jamal anything. But she still felt a tad guilty. "Because after I left here, I realized that I didn't want to leave."

"Just like that? All on your own, you came to realize this?"

Another flicker of guilt whizzed through her. Did he suspect something? No, she was being paranoid. There was no way he could.

"Yes."

He stared intently at her, then looked away, as if something he saw there bothered him. "Earlier, in the bar—"

"Shhhhh," Sharice said, not wanting to talk about anything serious that might ruin her resolve to stay here with him. Moving her hand lower, brushing the hair that had teased her when

138

he'd come to the door, moving even lower, she wrapped her fingers around his cock.

She squeezed.

He gasped.

Sharice raised up and placed her mouth against his, brushing a soft kiss against his lips. "Let's talk later, okay?"

"Alright." Jamal put his hand behind her neck, and pulled her to him. His mouth, once again moving firmly over hers, answered her question. There'd be no talking right now. Not communication that involved logical, rational thought, anyway—which was good because Sharice didn't think she was capable of forming complex sentences—or even simple sentences involving more than two words.

As Jamal's mouth plundered hers and his hands roved her side, she rolled on top of him. Just as she'd imagined being when she'd been on the phone with Shawn.

Only this felt better. Much better. Her hips pressed against his hips, her chest brushed against his chest, teasing her nipples to instant hardness. His hands pulled her body to him, as if he couldn't get close enough. His tongue explored her mouth as if he could not taste enough.

Jamal made her feel as if he could never get enough. Of *all* of her.

Which drove her need higher.

Jamal made her feel cherished.

Which made her heart race.

Jamal made her feel special.

Breaking the kiss, Sharice raised her hips off of him, reached for his cock and placed him between her legs, positioning him right where she wanted him.

While staring into his eyes, Sharice lowered her hips. Jamal glided inside of her, hitting the spot deep within her that made her gasp.

Jamal's eyes turned two shades darker, seeming to lose focus. His lips parted and he moaned, his grip on her ass tightening. "Oh, baby. You feel so good."

"Yeah . . ." was all she could manage. She felt breathless.

Sharice lifted her hips and tore her gaze from his, looking down to where their bodies were connected.

That's what she felt. A connection.

She pumped her hips. Up and down. Slow and then fast.

Once again, Jamal's grip on her hips tightened. This time, to stop her. "Don't move. I can't—"

Sharice stopped long enough to take his hands from her hips and place them by his head, holding them captive.

She shimmied against him.

"Baby." His tone pleaded.

"Jamal." Her tone demanded. "This is what I want."

She squeezed his hands. "Your touch."

She gyrated her hips. "Your desire."

Jamal exhaled heavily.

Sharice leaned down, pressing her mouth against his. "Your kiss. I want all of you."

Jamal groaned. Jerking his hands out from under hers, he placed a hand on the back of her head and pulled her hard against him. His kiss was no longer gentle. It demanded and possessed, his tongue restlessly exploring her mouth, constantly roving as if desperate to discover any secrets that might be hidden there.

Sharice let him explore, meeting his tongue, mating with his mouth, holding nothing back, exposing her secrets—her want, her desire, all for his taking.

His hands moved back to her hips, pushing them up, pulling them down, guiding her faster, urging her deeper.

The familiar heat spread through her body, rushing down-ward—from her heart to her stomach, upward—from her toes to her thighs, growing hotter.

Jamal's fingers dug into her ass cheeks.

"Now. Please." His voice was pained.

"Now." Her voice was joyous.

"Yes," he said, his body going still while his cock throbbed inside her.

"Yes," she said, her muscles clenching and unclenching around his cock.

They clung to each other, riding the tide of passion together.

As her breathing became regular and her body no longer quaked, Sharice raised her head to look at Jamal. His eyes were closed and a faint smile played on his lips.

She dropped her head back onto his chest.

His hand lightly rubbed her back.

"That was fantastic but . . . please tell me we're done for a bit," she said.

His laughter rumbling against her chest was the last sound she remembered hearing before she fell asleep.

Sharice tiptoed to the bedroom door, then turned back for yet another peek. After propping herself on an elbow and watching Jamal sleep for a good fifteen minutes after she'd woken up, she still could not get enough of seeing him.

This time, he was flat on his stomach, his arms thrown out from his sides, the sheet tangled around his legs and covering only his ass.

Sharice licked her lips. If she wasn't running late, she'd go back and slide under the covers, rubbing her hips against his delectable ass, while kissing his neck, his back, before slipping her hands underneath him, searching for his cock—

Her panties felt wet.

Sharice grinned, blew him a kiss, and headed out the door. She'd see him again. She—

Stopped.

Hmmmm.

It didn't feel right to just leave Jamal without a word, like he was just another one-night stand. Something was going on here. Something scary and exciting that she didn't want to put a label on, or think too much about. Something that required her to do more than just skip out on Jamal without a word.

Sharice walked through the dining room to the desk in the corner of the room. Opening the drawer, she removed a piece of hotel stationery, grabbed a pen, and began writing. Finished, she folded the paper and returned to the bedroom.

Jamal was still comatose.

As she reread her note, it dawned on her that this was the first time she'd told Jamal her name. How backward was that? The one guy she cared about hadn't known her name.

Well, he did now.

Smiling, she placed the note on the pillow next to Jamal and kissed his cheek lightly. As she turned to leave, Dr. Love's words flashed through her mind: *Go sin*.

She smiled. Yeah, well, she'd already sinned. Big time.

6

Sharice sat on the four-foot tall barstool, staring at the menu spread open in front of her on the oval table. It felt odd to be at Club Maxwell's in the early evening—she'd always meant to try out the food, but had never been there at dinner time.

Tonight, she had a reason to be there at dinner time. She had a date . . . with Jamal. When was the last time that she'd been out on something as simple, as innocent as a date?

She suppressed a dopey grin—something that she'd found herself having to do ever since she'd left Jamal in the morning. In the midst of preparing her PowerPoint slides for a presentation for an investor meeting, she'd stared blankly at the screen, reliving the feel of Jamal underneath her, thrusting inside of her slowly, then quickly, changing his motion from the usual in-and-out to circular gyrations.

Who would've guessed that the simple, easy motions could've brought her to climax like that?

This time, she couldn't prevent the silly grin from spreading over her face.

"I've never seen anyone that happy about our menu," said a cheery voice.

Busted.

Sharice raised her eyes to the woman standing before her, notepad poised between her red-tipped fingertips. Amusement shone in her eyes.

"Uh. I was thinking of something else."

The woman smiled, obviously deciding that further commentary would constitute prying. "Are you ready to order?"

"No, not yet. I'm waiting for someone."

"Sure. Take your time."

Sharice watched the young woman walk away, a definite swish to her strut. Maybe she'd gotten some this morning, too.

The thought caused Sharice's dopey grin to grow wider.

Smiling was the last thing she thought she'd be doing. The fact that her worst fear had just come true—that she would, indeed, be calling into Dr. Love and reporting her sin, the desire for a r-e-l-a-t-i-o-n-s-h-i-p—should have had her paralyzed by fear.

But, instead of feeling afraid, she felt alive, excited. Though she didn't know how long this feeling would last or what the future—if any—held for her and Jamal, she wanted to revel in the feeling. It'd been so long. It'd taken so long to put her heart back together after Malcolm, then Darrell, she'd been unwilling to risk it again.

Until Jamal.

Maybe three was, indeed, the charm. Maybe Jamal would, indeed, prove to be different.

The front door opened. She glanced that way, hoping to see Jamal. It wasn't him but the dark-skinned brotha with the locks looked familiar.

Sharice frowned. Where had she seen him before? At Geoffrey's? At Maxwell's? At—

That was it—outside of Maxwell's. It was Shawn.

Damn. Maybe he'd turn and walk in the opposite direction.

He turned and walked her way.

Maybe he wouldn't see her.

He looked in her direction and paused by her table. His lips curved into a sexy smile.

Her smile was polite. "Hi, Shawn."

His smile slipped. Confusion skittered across his brow. "Do I know you?"

"Sharice."

"Sharice . . . ?"

Sharice frowned. What game was he playing? "We . . . 'spoke' earlier."

"Baby, if you and I spoke, I'd remember."

"Come on. I called you at . . ." Sharice bent down and retrieved her cell phone. She flipped it open and brought up the last call she'd made to Shawn. ". . . at 3:47 A.M. 510-555-9123."

"My number is 510-555-9124."

Sharice's heart raced. Maybe she misheard. "Your number's not 510-555-9123?"

"No . . . Did we meet?"

Sharice stared sightlessly into Shawn's eyes. "I'm sorry . . . I don't mean to be rude but I . . . need to sort this out."

"Hey, maybe I can . . . you know, help you sort things out."

Sharice smiled politely. "No. Thank you."

His smile was sexy. "Sure, babe. Wish it had been me. If you change your mind, call me."

Shawn winked and walked on.

Sharice sat back and closed her eyes.

If she hadn't been talking to Shawn, who the hell had she been calling? Opening her eyes, she jerked upright, opened her cell, and called up the number she thought was Shawn's. As she hit the dial button and the phone began to ring, Jamal slid onto the stool next to her.

"Hey," he said, smiling. He leaned forward and pressed a light kiss against her lips.

"Hey," she said, forcing a smile and debating whether or not to disconnect the call. It wasn't as if she could talk to whomever answered with Jamal right here in front of her.

The phone rang in her ear.

Jamal's phone rang.

She'd just give it one more ring, see if voicemail answered, see if—by some miracle—the greeting had been changed to say his name.

Idly, she glanced over at Jamal.

He was staring at the display of his phone, stunned.

"Is everything okay?" Sharice asked.

Jamal looked up at her, his eyes filled with surprise, shock, and . . . guilt?

"What's wrong?" she asked, deciding the Shawn-who-was-not-Shawn thing could wait.

Jamal's gaze went back to his cell phone.

Sharice disconnected the call.

Jamal's phone died in mid-ring.

While her mind raced at warp speed to put together the puzzle pieces flying through her brain, her eyes seemed to take in Jamal's actions in slow motion.

He flipped his now-silent cell phone closed.

He rubbed the side of the phone with his thumb, not looking at her.

Finally, he returned his gaze to her, his look apologetic.

The puzzle pieces instantly fell into place. "You. It's been you—"

"I can explain."

"Really? Why start now?" She tossed her cell phone into her purse with more force than was necessary. "I can't fucking believe this."

"Sharice, I was going to tell you—"

"When? When were you going to tell me, Jamal?"

"Last night, at the bar. Then, afterwards, in—"

The blood roared past her eardrums, heated her body, and produced a shakiness that made her want to reach out and break something.

Like Jamal's neck.

She spread her hands out in front of her. "So this has all been some sick joke?"

"No!"

"Why? I just want to know why?"

"Look, it's not the way—"

"Oh, forget it." Sharice yanked her purse from the arm of the chair and jumped off of the barstool. "I don't want to know. It doesn't matter."

Jamal reached out a hand, stopping her. "Would you just give me a chance to explain?"

Explain what? How she'd just been made an ass out of?

Again.

How she'd picked the wrong guy to trust?

Again.

What the fuck was wrong with her? Women were credited with intuition that was supposed to guide them to making the right decisions in life. Well, she'd really tried to listen to hers this time. Though, obviously, she must be the only woman born with no intuition.

Or hers was broken.

Sharice jerked her arm out of his grasp.

"Please." The word was issued between gritted teeth.

Oh, geez. As painful as it might be, she really did want to know why, really did want to know what the hell was going on.

"Fine." She plopped back on the stool, crossed her arms, and tapped her fingertips against her forearm.

Jamal looked like he wanted to roll his eyes. He frowned, instead. "Look, let's calm down. I know I should've told you sooner—"

"Sooner?"

This time, he did roll his eyes. "I know I should've told you. But I didn't want to lose you—"

"And that made it okay to lie to me? To pretend to be two people?"

"I only *pretended* to be one person."

"Yeah, well, you pretended to be Shawn and lured me into phone sex with you. Then, as Jamal, had real sex with me." Sharice felt righteous. "Anyway you look at it, you lied."

Jamal's lips tightened. His nostrils flared. "Yeah, well, you lied, too. You had phone sex with Shawn right after having real sex with me." He flung his hands out, like a magician after making a rabbit disappear. "And you didn't tell me. A lie by omission."

Sharice opened her mouth, then closed it.

He had a point. She did lie. When he'd asked her why she'd come back to him, she hadn't mentioned Shawn. Technically, she didn't have to tell him. But in her heart, she'd felt she should've. "You're right. I'm sorry."

But that still didn't excuse him, absolve him of any wrongdoing. That didn't mean he still wasn't wrong for pretending to be Shawn, for leading her on, for—

"I was wrong," Jamal said.

Oh. Okay.

"When I got your first message, I loved your voice. It was sultry, sexy . . ."

Ah, that's nice.

". . . a porn star's voice."

"What?"

"Will you let me finish?"

But, a porn star's voice? Sharice sighed.

"You sounded classy."

A *classy* porn star?

"I'd gotten other calls from women, looking for Shawn, and none of them sounded like you. When I called you back, I was going to tell you not to waste your time with Shawn, that he was a playa . . ." He shrugged. "But then, I heard your voice, and I wanted to meet you. Tell you in person."

"Why didn't you?"

"Because when I met you, I realized you liked playas."

"I don't like playas."

He raised a brow.

"I don't." She didn't like playas. She simply chose them because she understood them; they were comfortable.

They weren't like Jamal.

"Well. I knew you wouldn't go for me. I'm not flashy. I don't do casual sex—usually. But, when you seemed interested in me and since you didn't know I was 'Shawn,' there didn't seem to be a reason to tell you."

"Why didn't you tell me when I called you, after I left the hotel?"

"Because I was angry, that you chose Shawn over me, a casual fuck over what I thought I could give you."

Oh. So she wasn't the only one who felt vulnerable in all this.

Sharice reached for his hand. "I didn't want that. I wanted you but . . . I was afraid of you, of feeling. Shawn was what I was used to, but—" Sharice rubbed her fingers across his skin, momentarily distracted by how good he felt, how good his hands had made her feel as he'd touched her body, strummed her—

"But?"

She turned her attention back to the conversation. "But I wasn't into him. All I could think about was you."

Jamal grinned. "I know. You said my name."

Sharice punched his arm.

He mimicked her voice. "'Oh, Jamal'. . .'Oh, Jamal.'"

149

Sharice laughed and socked him again. "Stop it."

"Okay, okay." The laughter faded from his eyes. "Sorry, aw'ight?"

"Yeah," she said softly.

"Let's start again. Hi, I'm Jamal." He stuck out his hand.

Sharice slipped her hand in his. "Hi, I'm Sharice."

"Nice to meet you, Sharice."

He placed a finger under her chin and tipped her head up, seconds before lowering his mouth to hers. Her tongue dipped between his lips, stealing a taste.

A taste of forgiveness and promise and beginnings.

The sound of a throat being cleared caused her to break away. She looked up into the amused expression of a guy with locks. "Got everything sorted out?" he asked.

"Yeah," she said.

"Okay," he winked and clapped Jamal on the back. "You're a lucky brotha," he said and walked away.

Jamal frowned. "Who was that?"

"Shawn."

"Shawn!"

Sharice told him what happened. When she finished, he said, "So that's your type. Pretty boys in designer suits and fancy cars?"

"Jamal, I explained why I went after guys like Shawn. I don't care about material things."

"Really?" He asked, his eyes sparkling.

"Really," she said, frowning.

"Okay, then. Let's go somewhere else to eat. I'll drive."

"Okay," she said, her tone slightly confused. He grabbed her hand and led her out the door and down the street, stopping in front of a red car.

Sharice took one look at the "vintage" Toyota Camry and burst out laughing. Turning to Jamal, she gave him a kiss.

"Yeah, I think you're my type."

Alyssa

A Sinful Proposition

1

"*Today* is the day to 'sin,'" Alyssa James said as she plopped down onto the lime green micro-suede chair in her best friend's office. She stared at Shannon, waiting for her response.

"You've got to stop listening to that garbage on the radio," Shannon said absently, not bothering to look up from whatever she was doing on her cranberry red VAIO.

"*The Sin Club* is not garbage. Dr. Love has successful sinners on his show every night. Today is my day."

"You've said that every day for the last 30 days."

"It's the power of positive thinking. I feel that *today* is going to be different."

Shannon shook her head. "How would you even know if you're sinning, Alyssa? You already break all the rules on your online blog."

Shannon had a point. Alyssa had started her blog, Sex in San Francisco, as a joke—she'd grabbed her camera and hit the streets of San Francisco, looking for interesting occurrences to write about. In a park in Pacific Heights, she'd snapped a photo of two dogs—a perfectly coiffed Jack Russell terrier and a scruffy mongrel of unidentifiable heritage—in *flagrante delicto*. Afterward, she'd blogged about how opposites attract, even in the animal kingdom.

How was she to know that Fifi belonged to a prominent politician's wife? And how could she have guessed that the wife would call every radio and television station demanding that Fifi's photo be removed? Alyssa hadn't removed the photo, instead encouraging visitors to participate in the fracas online.

Sex in San Francisco was proof that *all* publicity was good publicity. Alyssa now dished the scoop on the private lives of San Francisco's rich and beautiful. But at a price. Hanging out in bushes and crashing parties left little time for a life of her own. So, while she did, indeed, "sin" for Sex in San Francisco, she had no time for personal sinning.

"I'm talking about sinning in my personal life."

"What personal life?"

"The personal life I'm about to have. I hired an assistant."

"That just means that you'll find more work for both of you to do."

While Alyssa didn't blame Shannon for her skepticism, a little best-friend humoring would've been nice. The negative energy rolling off of Shannon in waves was starting to put a dent in her conviction that today was *the* day.

She sighed. Loudly.

Shannon finally looked up and asked with resignation, "So what personal sin are you finally going to commit today?"

Alyssa grinned. "I'm glad you asked. I'm thinking about sex. After all, shouldn't the blogger of Sex in San Francisco be having sex?"

"Umm-hmm." Shannon's gaze returned to her computer.

"Yeah, I know. I've always been a commitment gal—"

"An understatement," Shannon said. "Three years with Phil, four years with that loser from high school, four years—"

"Well, now I'm thinking, the heck with that. I can't afford the time for a relationship."

"Especially," Shannon muttered, "with the emotionally needy guys you get involved with."

Alyssa ignored that. "But I have time for a fling. If I'm willing to sin. That is, just go up to a hot guy and proposition him."

Shannon snorted. "Now, that I'd like to see. In fact, I'd pay to see that—you propositioning someone."

"Very funny." Alyssa decided to change the subject. "So how's business at The Perfect Date?"

"Slow. You know how tough startups are."

"Yeah."

"If I don't get a burst of business soon, I'm afraid . . ." Shannon sighed. After a minute, she beamed, instantly transformed into the poster child for positive thinking. "But I got a new client today." Once again, she tore her eyes away from her computer screen. "You won't believe who called me to hire a *corporate* escort!"

Alyssa smiled. Shannon always emphasized the word "corporate" lest anyone think she dealt in sexscorts—a term she coined for the less reputable escort services.

"Barney," said Alyssa.

"Barney Gaffney? Why would he need my services?"

"No. I meant Barney, from television. And I can think of one hundred reasons as to why he'd need your services. One, he's dull. Two, he lumbers around—"

Shannon sighed heavily.

Alyssa smiled. "Okay, okay. I'll be serious. Who?"

Before she could answer, the phone rang and Shannon answered. Nanoseconds later, she grinned. "Please send him in, Charlotte."

Shannon stood up.

Alyssa gathered her purse and prepared to stand.

"No. Don't go. I want you to see this."

Alyssa shrugged and settled back into her chair.

The elation in Shannon's face suddenly faded and she directed a stern look at Alyssa. "You *cannot* put this on your gossip blog."

Indignation rumbled in Alyssa's stomach. "I do not deal in gossip. I deal in facts and—"

"Alyssa!"

"Of course I won't. You know I never write about personal or confidential—"

The soft whoosh of the office door opening, coupled with the ass-kissing grin spreading across Shannon's face, stopped Alyssa in mid-protest. Alyssa turned toward the door, desperate to see who could bring such an abomination to the mouth of her no-nonsense friend.

"Mr. Brooks. Please come in," Shannon gushed behind her.

The Mr. Brooks—as in, Tony Alfonso Brooks . . . as in, owner of Flush, The Gilded Cage, Bubbles, and a dozen other upscale bars . . . as in the very single, very sexy, Antonio Banderas clone whose private life was a mystery.

And here she'd been given a glimpse into that mystery . . . That the most eligible man in The City apparently had to pay to get a date. Priceless. Glee bubbled up inside her. What a great story this would—

Damn. There was no story. She'd just promised Shannon she wouldn't write about him.

How could Shannon do this to me?

Just last week, Alyssa had written a piece speculating on the likelihood that Tony Brooks and supermodel-turned-restaurateur Chantelle Dubois had eloped to Sarlat, France.

Obviously that wasn't true, since he was standing in front of her. So putting Mr. Brooks within touching distance but saying she couldn't write about him was like . . . like . . . putting a fudge sundae in front of a child and saying, "don't eat it."

As Tony glided into the room in a navy Versace suit,

Alyssa's racing heart, fluttery stomach, and rise in body temperature told her that he was like a fudge sundae in other ways—delicious, decadent, and deadly.

"Shannon, thanks for seeing me on such short notice." Smiling, he extended his hand to Shannon.

"My pleasure. Before we begin, let me introduce you to Alyssa James."

No, no. Don't introduce me.

". . . Alyssa, this is Mr. Tony Brooks."

Just this once, why hadn't Alyssa listened to her mother? When Alyssa was a teenager, her mom had always stressed to never leave the house without looking one's absolute best. Well, today Alyssa had left the house looking her absolute worst—no makeup, ponytail looped through the back of a "Just Do It" black Nike baseball cap, olive green cargo pants. The only item of clothing saving her from total fashion disaster was her fuchsia Bebe T-shirt.

Tony seemed to agree, for his eyes lingered on her breasts.

Alyssa blushed.

His gaze returned to her face. "She's not quite what I expected but . . . the blond hair and blue eyes definitely work."

Alyssa's mouth dropped open.

Tony's gaze dropped to her mouth. "Nice, pouty lips. A little glossy stuff would help."

Glossy stuff? The nerve, utter gall. Why—

His gaze traveled lower. "Great breasts . . ."

Alyssa's face felt crimson. "How—"

"Kind of hard to make out the rest of her in those unattractive pants, but I'm guessing she's about a size eight?"

Once again, his eyes returned to her face. He raised a brow, as if expecting an answer.

I'm a size six. Alyssa's lips tightened.

His gaze returned to her lips.

Maybe he was imagining them coated in "glossy stuff." Or

maybe he was imagining the feel of them against his, pressing and nibbling, while her hand caressed his Michelangelo-carved cheeks, before she trailed her fingers to his black, satiny, shoulder-length hair, freeing it from the band that held it, running her fingers—

No. That was her imagination, not his. Silly twit.

Her jaw clenched. "Would you like to see my teeth, Mr. Brooks?"

He seemed to consider the question. "I hadn't thought about it, but it might be a good idea—"

"I am not a horse, Mr. Brooks, and I find your—"

Shannon's laugh had an edge of hysteria. "Don't you just love her sense of humor?"

His eyes narrowed, no longer seeming to assess horseflesh, instead searching for a hint of the sense of humor Shannon had promised.

Alyssa smiled, careful to hide all her teeth.

"Why, just before you arrived we were discussing how *today* was her day."

Alyssa looked at Shannon, whose smile was one step away from a grimace. *Don't fuck this up for me*, her look said.

Don't fuck what up? Alyssa shot back. *I don't know what the hell is going on here. One second I'm talking about* The Sin Club *and the next minute I'm being stripped and*—

Her words echoed in her mind: *Today is the day to "sin."* Shannon was trying to remind her of that.

Alyssa's eyes widened. She jerked her head in Tony's direction. "*You* want me to be his date?"

"You hadn't figured that out?" asked Tony.

"No. I'm not a—"

Tony grinned. "Then you're perfect." He turned back to Shannon. "I'll take her."

2

I'll take her.

Alyssa glared at Shannon. Shannon held her gaze for a second, then rounded her desk and walked toward Tony. She slipped her professional mask back into place.

"Mr. Brooks, maybe you ought to consider a couple of other candidates." She took his arm and drew him toward the outer office. "I've got some books with photos and bios."

"Shannon, I've made up my mind." He motioned behind him, in Alyssa's direction. "I want her."

"Okay, then I'll just have you fill out some paperwork." Shannon ushered him out of the office. At the door, she paused and looked back at Alyssa. *I'll be back*, she mouthed, then turned away.

Oh, yes, Shannon would definitely be back. There were a couple of little things they needed to discuss.

I'll take her.

Bartered for like a sack of flour, that's how those words had made her feel. Alyssa tucked a loose strand of hair behind her ear and watched Tony through the glass office door. So confident, so arrogant.

I'll take her.

So exciting.

Those words shouldn't thrill her, but they did. They ought to offend her. But now as she stared through the glass at the sexy man sitting there, talking with Shannon, she reconsidered.

"Maybe I'll take you," she whispered. On the plush beige carpet covering Shannon's office, or the outer office, or the elevator . . .

Sinful images flickered through her mind. Images of his finely tailored suit jacket lying crumpled at his feet. The white shirt unbuttoned to the waistband of his pants. A noticeable bulge decorating his perfectly pleated slacks . . .

And as Alyssa slides up to him, she's dressed only in his scarlet and black paisley tie, his eyes rove her body. No longer wearing the analytical gaze of an experienced horse trader, his eyes glisten with lust as he reaches for her, pulling her close, letting the friction of his shirt against her skin turn her nipples to hard pebbles, and the feel of his hard cock against her naked pussy—

"Stop looking at him like that," Shannon snapped, coming back into the office and checking that the glass door was locked.

Alyssa blinked.

She was no longer naked. Tony no longer had a hard-on.

She turned to Shannon. "Stop looking at him like what?"

"Like . . . you want to sin with him!"

"But I do want to sin with him."

"You can't."

Alyssa frowned. "What do you mean, I can't? Didn't you just remind me that today was my day, in front of him?"

"Yes, and it is your day—to help me now and sin later. The

160

Perfect Date does not employ prostitutes, call girls, or sexcorts. We are a 'corporate' escort service."

"Technically, I'm not an escort. So why can't I have sex with him?"

"Technically, you *will* be an escort. Alyssa, I could get my business license revoked, not to mention have some sort of criminal charges filed against me if the state found out my employees were having sex with clients." Shannon's voice was panicked.

"All right, all right," Alyssa muttered. "What else would I have to do? Not that I've agreed to do anything yet."

Shannon's smile was weak. "Oh, just be agreeable and friendly and . . . a perfect date."

"That's it?"

"Yeah, pretty much."

Alyssa tapped her finger against her chin. "And I can have sex with him after the date?"

"Yes."

Surely she could resist him for twenty-four hours.

Alyssa grinned. "I'll take him."

3

Alyssa stared out the window of Tony's Mercedes convertible, ignoring the landscape. Instead, her thoughts were on her dilemma. Apparently, resisting Tony was going to be harder than she'd thought.

When Shannon had told him that Alyssa would be his date, Tony had turned his megawatt smile on her—and her stomach had flopped and her panties had felt wet.

When he'd taken her arm to escort her out of the office, his firm grip had sent her mind back to the fantasy—making her imagine his fingertips on her naked flesh and his body heat as he'd reached around in front of her to open the door for her—she'd wanted to lean back, press herself against him, and make his cock as hard as she'd imagined.

I'll take her.

Well, she couldn't stop wanting to take *him*. In Shannon's office. In the elevator that had whisked them down to the garage. In the car that they were in right now.

Well, maybe not right now, since they were speeding down

Highway 101 toward the coastal town of Mendocino at what had to be 120 miles per hour.

But she'd like to have him pull over to the side of the road, and then she'd lean over and trace his jaw with her fingertip.

"Do you know what I'm going to do to you?" she'd whisper throatily in his ear.

She'd run her hand down the front of his slacks, finding the zipper and pulling it down, before finding *him*.

She'd laugh sexily. "I see you do know what I'm going to do to you."

She'd take his cock in her hand.

He'd gasp.

She'd turn all the way toward him and climb over the gearshift, climb onto his lap and his hands would grip her ass, pulling her, guiding her—

"... all right?"

Alyssa snapped her head from the pasture blurring in front of her eyes and looked at him. Loose strands of his hair danced in the breeze from the top-down convertible. She let her eyes travel over the chiseled jaw that she'd just touched in her mind.

He turned to look at her.

She blushed. *Get a grip, Alyssa.* "I'm sorry. My mind . . ." *was on straddling you, putting your cock inside me, and—* ". . . wandered."

"I asked if you were all right."

Had she lost all of her pride?

It was bad enough that she was feeling lust for a man who viewed her as chattel, but surely she could manage to pay attention and string together a coherent sentence. After all, she was supposed to be a professional "corporate" escort.

Alyssa cleared her throat and summoned the experienced escort from deep within. "Yes, I'm fine."

His long lean fingers—the same ones she'd imagined holding her ass—moved to the radio. "Would you like to listen to music?" he asked, pressing a button on the radio at the same time.

Whatever you like—that's what Shannon would tell her to say.

A replay of a prior *Sin Club* radio episode filled the air.

"Anything but that," Alyssa muttered.

"You don't like *The Sin Club*?"

No. Today she did not like Dr. Love. Yes, she was sinning because of him. But couldn't she have chosen a better guy to sin with? One who didn't view her as . . . livestock? One she hadn't just profiled on her Web site?

Whatever you like.

She made a sound that he could take either way.

Tony's tone was amused. "You must be the only woman in the nation who doesn't like the show."

And you're probably an expert on most of the women in the nation, aren't you?

". . . So, what was your sin, Sharice?" asked Dr. Love, his unique deep voice oozing sexiness from Tony's speakers.

"I was unhappy with the brothas I was meeting, so I decided to call Shawn, this man I'd met—a new experience for me," said a sultry feminine voice.

"Your first sin. Good. Go on."

"Only, I unknowingly misdialed. Jamal called me back, but I thought he was Shawn, and we made arrangements to meet for drinks. Shawn didn't show up, but I met Jamal, not knowing he was also Shawn . . ."

"Uh, Sharice? This is a bit hard to follow. What's your sin?"

"Oh. Right. My second sin was I had phone sex—"

Dr. Love laughed. "You go, girl."

Tony laughed. "Now, *that's* a sin."

Alyssa inhaled sharply at Tony's words. The admiration in

his tone indicated approval. Did he like phone sex? Now, there was an idea. Of calling him up and teasing him with some of the titillating thoughts running through her mind. Since phone sex wasn't exactly sex, maybe it wasn't banned in the "corporate" escort bylaws.

". . . and my last sin, well, I let go of my fear, and gave into a relationship."

Did every person who called in to Dr. Love have sins that led to a relationship? What about those who were looking for hot sex with a gorgeous, successful man who made your insides—

"Have you sinned, Alyssa?" asked Tony.

His words yanked her back to the present. "What?"

Tony grinned. "Too personal?"

That was an understatement. Nothing but sins had been running through her mind from the moment she'd met him.

"All right, I guess so. We'll start with something easier. Do you have a boyfriend?"

"Uh, no."

"I imagine being a Perfect Date keeps you pretty busy."

"Uh, no. I just started at The Perfect Date."

This time, his smile was sexy. "So I'm your first?"

Alyssa's stomach flipped over. "Yes."

His eyes took a quick tour of her body before he returned his gaze to the road. "I'll do what I can to make your first time good."

Oh, God. He did not just say that.

Her mind instantly zoomed to their imaginery first time. Of her on top of him, looking down into those intense gray eyes glazed by the need she ignited in him. Her hips would move slowly on his cock as she stared into his eyes, watching the desire become need and—

And whatever you do, no sex, Alyssa, Shannon had said. . . . *if the state found out my employees were having sex with clients . . .*

Oh, God. How could Shannon say that?

Well, "the state" wasn't in the car with them right now. And she'd be willing to bet no ménage with state officials was being planned for them tonight.

Alyssa sighed, regretting that she had agreed to this "sin." No sex with the sexiest, wealthiest, most sought after man in the Bay Area. No inside scoop on the sexiest, wealthiest, most sought after man in the Bay Area for her avid readers.

How the hell was she going to avoid both of those no-nos? If a miracle occurred and she did, Shannon was going to owe her for the rest of their lives.

Alyssa stared at his profile, noticing that not only was his hair longer than any man's she'd ever been with, so were his eyelashes. If not for the masculine jawline, the slight bump in his nose that hinted at a long-ago break, he'd be almost perfect.

An almost perfect date.

Yeah, well, that was a first, too—being with a man who was prettier than she was. Not that she was Salma Hayek or anything, but she could hold her own at Hooters. But, being with a man—

"Did Shannon tell you what you need to do?"

"Yes." *Whatever you like. And no sex.* Alyssa suppressed a sigh. "But it would be helpful to hear it from you."

He changed lanes and passed a slow-moving SUV before continuing. "I made an offer on a nightclub called Strands, but the owner, Giovanni Maffucci—"

"Giovanni Maffucci, the . . ." *sleaze bucket whom she'd written about on Sex in San Francisco?* ". . . guy who owns the string of strip clubs?"

Tony shot her an admiring glance.

Alyssa puffed up with pride—and lust—which instantly dissolved into apprehension. Were they going to meet Giovanni?

She couldn't meet Giovanni. He might recognize her. He—

Wait a minute. The odds of him recognizing her were right up there with Tony falling in love with her. There was no photo of her on her Web site. And she couldn't remember a photo of her ever being published. Plus, he wouldn't recognize her name, since she wrote her entries under the name of Erica Allen.

She was safe from love and discovery.

"Yes. Well, he's playing two ends against the middle. He's invited those who've made offers to his estate. This weekend it's my turn."

Tony's kissable lips twisted. "He wants to get to know us so he can choose the best man for Strands."

"You don't believe him?"

He shrugged. "It's not a question of belief. It's a question of business."

"I'm not sure I understand."

"Giovanni is choosing a buyer based on emotional criteria." He turned from the road, his gray eyes burning Alyssa in their intensity.

Her breath froze in her chest.

"Business is about making the best deal. Emotion has no place in the transaction."

"Oh . . ."

He turned back to the road.

She let the breath leak from her lungs.

The steeliness underlying his tone implied that he was talking about more than this business deal—that there were other areas in his life where emotion didn't belong. Had some woman broken his heart?

Alyssa almost snorted at the thought. More likely he'd broken a string of hearts. All a woman had to do was look into those gray eyes that made her feel like the center of his universe, or see his sexy lips parted in a smile that melted the panties right off her hips and sent flutters—

"... and just smile vacantly, stare adoringly at me, pay attention to my every word ..."

The sudden awareness of his words pushed all thought of thongs and illicit flutters from her mind.

Did he just say what she thought he did?

"You want me to play a brainless ... ditz?"

A frown marred his perfectly smooth brow. "Of course."

Of course?!

"Shannon said she'd tell you all this."

Oh, just be agreeable and friendly and ... a perfect date, Shannon had said. No wonder the look on her face had been odd—a cross between indigestion and excess gas.

"She expressed it a tad differently."

"Is there a problem?" That steely, icy business tone was back. The one that said there'd better not be a problem.

"No," she lied.

"Good." His frown disappeared. "Giovanni is a notorious male chauvinist. An intelligent date would convince him I was not the right man for Strands." The last sentence dripped with disdain, though from the date part or the being thought of as the wrong man, she couldn't tell.

"And Giovanni likes blondes?"

Tony turned toward her. This time, his smile caused shivers to prickle her skin. "No. *I* like blondes." His gaze dropped, lingering on her breasts, reminding her that he thought she had great breasts.

Her face heated. Her nipples tightened.

His smile seemed knowing as he turned back to the road.

"And do you like brainless women?" She was pleased to hear the amusement in her tone.

"No. Ditzes are not my type."

"Then what is your type?" Her voice sounded sultry, kind of like that woman—what was her name? Sharice?—on Dr. Love's show. A sinning voice.

Shannon would disapprove.

Tony's look said he approved. "I'm into women with brains."

"As long as they have great breasts," she quipped.

He shot another lingering look at hers. His smile was sly. "That does help . . ."

Alyssa's breasts tingled as if he'd reached over and touched them. She wished he *would* reach over and touch them, first slipping his hand under her shirt and . . .

She had to stop letting her thoughts drift down the road to sex—a road that had a huge barricade blocking all traffic for the duration of this trip.

Alyssa sighed.

They rode in silence for a couple miles. The covert glances she sent Tony's way showed him to be the picture of relaxation—his hand tapped the gearshift lightly and his head bobbed slightly, both keeping the beat to a Keith Urban song coming through the speakers. His gaze occasionally left the road to glance at the wildflowers starting to bloom along the side of the highway or a barn in the distance or . . . whatever.

Over on her side of the car, Alyssa's body felt as tense as an arched bow. Tony's body heat was like an invisible caress, enveloping her, tickling her skin, and injecting an overdose of hormones into her veins. And his comments that hinted at the fact that he was attracted to her encouraged her fantasies to saturate her mind.

She frowned.

And just why was he insinuating that he found her attractive—well, at least certain parts of her?

He had stressed that her purpose here was business. If that

was the case, wouldn't he have picked a woman who appealed to Giovanni Maffucci, a woman who didn't have to pretend to be a ditz?

That, coupled with his comments, proved that his "hints" were real. He must find her attractive. Despite her "unattractive pants." Despite—

Oh, no. She didn't have an adequate wardrobe for hobknobbing with big—sleazy?—dealmakers. Maybe she should ask if they could stop somewhere to pick up a couple of dresses and some shoes.

"Mr. Brooks—"

He waved a hand. "Don't call me Mr. Brooks. It's Tony—No . . ." He paused before continuing. "We need something more . . . intimate . . ." He snapped his fingers. "You'll be Lissy."

She was appalled. "Lissy?"

"And you'll call me Tonykins."

"Tonykins!"

Tonykins shot her a grin.

Lissy groaned.

What had she gotten herself into?

4

As Alyssa stared in horror at the clothing spread over the bed in the guest suite she and Tony would be sharing at Giovanni's estate, she began to understand exactly what she'd gotten herself into:

T-r-o-u-b-l-e.

She picked up one of the dresses Tony had bought for her. Holding the black material up to the light, she stretched it, hoping to make it expand.

She relaxed her grip.

The dress shrunk to its original Barbie-doll size.

"I can't wear this!"

Tony came up behind her. His suit jacket brushed her back as he reached forward, taking the dress from her.

His nearness called to her, making her want to forget the dress in front of her, forget about all types of clothing, instead stripping off their own clothing and adding it, one piece at a time, to those on the bed.

Tony flipped over the tag in the back of the garment. "Did I get you the wrong size?"

His breath caressed her ear.

She wanted to tilt her head to the side and move her ear to his lips.

His arm pressed against her shoulder.

She resisted the urge to run her fingers along his forearm, dipping her fingertips under his shirt cuff and teasing the sensitive skin at his wrist.

His chest touched her back.

One teeny tiny step backward and she'd feel his body pressed up against hers . . . A shimmy or two of her hips, and she might feel his cock harden against her ass . . . A 180-degree pivot would land her in his arms, pressed against his chest, chin length away from his kissable lips . . .

Alyssa forced thoughts of his nearness away and her attention went back to the dress in hand. "It's barely . . . there."

"Giovanni will like it." His tone was matter-of-fact.

Who cares?

"I like it." His tone was melted chocolate.

All righty, then. Now, I care. But still . . .

He lifted the dress by the straps. "Here. You hold it."

She took it from him.

"Now, place it against you."

Alyssa held it against her, pinning it to her shoulders with her fingertips.

"I think it'll fit you perfectly . . . here." Tony stretched the dress across her chest.

His chest pressed against her back.

Alyssa gasped.

Stretching the material and moving his hands down, his fingers grazed the outside of her breasts and wound around to her stomach.

"And it'll fit you perfectly here." His palms flattened against her stomach, pressing lightly.

His groin grazed her ass, just enough to let her know that his cock was hard, just enough to drive her wild with the desire to grind her hips against him.

And whatever you do, no sex, Alyssa.

She really did not think she was going to be able to keep that promise. Maybe Shannon would accept a compromise: Alyssa would have sex with Tony but she wouldn't write about him.

"Would you wear it for me?"

Oh, God. Right now, she felt like she would do anything for him. As long as it resulted in what her body was craving right this second. The feel of him inside her, her legs wrapped around his waist, her arms around his neck, his mouth suckling her nipples, while her hips pumped and his hips thrust . . .

Alyssa jerked away, desperate to break the pull of his body, his ability to send her into a sexual daze. She took a step toward safety—that is three steps forward and out of reach of his invisible caress—so that she could think.

When she turned around, Tony had moved and was leaning against the door frame of the open closet door. Arms crossed, legs crossed, amused expression, and . . . aroused.

"Okay. I'll wear the dress. But, that bed . . . "

Her gaze went to the king-size bed. This time, she ignored the clothing strewn across it, instead taking in the silk, brocade pillows of every size that were piled high on the mattress, while filmy gold material hung from the sides of the canopy, tied back with thick rope.

Rope.

That sent a whole other set of images through her mind, of Tony bound and helpless, waiting for her touch, straining forward for more as she teased and taunted him with her body and her tongue, stroking his cock just enough to keep him hot and ready, but making him wait. Making him moan—

". . . It's fit for a sultan," she finished.

"Would you like me to ask for different bedding?"

"No." Her gaze darted back to him.

His gaze was teasing.

"Tony, I cannot sleep with you in that bed."

"Then you don't have to sleep with me in that bed."

She nodded. "Good. Then I think we should ask for a roll-away . . . " Her voice trailed off as she realized he'd meant those words an entirely different way.

Amusement had fled from his face. His gaze was erotically serious.

He meant she could sleep—translation: have sex—with him anywhere she wanted. It didn't have to be in that bed.

Her heart pummeled her ribs.

"Tony, I'll be honest. I really want to have sex with you—"

"Great."

He walked toward her.

She put a hand out in front of her. Her hand trembled.

"I didn't mean now." Her voice shook.

He stopped in front of her and placed a hand at the back of her neck, his thumb under her chin, tilting her head up. His thumb caressed her chin. "Tonight then."

He lowered his head.

She turned her head.

His lips grazed her jaw.

"Oh!"

His mouth nibbled, working its way back to her mouth.

"We both signed a contract agreeing to no sex so if you are still interested in me after this 'date,' then I would like to have sex with you." The words came out in a rush—breathless and garbled—because of the blood pounding in her head, the shakiness invading her body, and the weakness that had seeped into her muscles, making it require all her concentration to stand upright and not press herself forward and send Tony backward, until he was sprawled under her on the bed.

There. She'd done it. Propositioned a hot guy for sex.

She'd sinned, just as she promised. And in a way that honored her agreement with Shannon.

She felt proud.

Well, she would've felt proud if Tony's lips hadn't moved to the corner of her mouth, hovering, waiting.

"Deal," he said. His breath teased her. "Seal it with a kiss."

Before she could think about the wisdom of solidifying a deal with a kiss, his mouth captured hers. His mouth moved slowly and thoroughly over hers, persuading a response from her.

His hand caressed her neck. His lips caressed her lips.

Alyssa surrendered, gave in to the pull.

She kissed him back. She slipped her hands underneath his suit jacket, slid them up his back, and pulled him closer, needing to feel her chest pressed against his.

He deepened the kiss, his lips no longer persuading, but seducing. His tongue no longer exploring, but plundering.

Alyssa moaned into his mouth.

He used the moan against her, taking it as a sign of permission. His hand slipped from her neck to her waist, pulling her hips against his, making her feel him, his need.

His thumbs caressed the skin under the hem of her T-shirt.

The voice of reason told her that the kiss was moving beyond the equivalent of a handshake, veering into a zone that was wild and carnal.

Stop, the little voice whispered in her head.

"You taste good," Tony whispered against her lips.

She liked Tony's whisper better than the voice in her head.

His mouth moved from hers, nibbling its way across her

jaw, to her ear. His hands slipped farther under her T-shirt, moving up her sides, his thumbs brushing the underside of her breasts.

Alyssa moaned again.

"You feel so good," he said.

Alyssa liked this whisper the best.

She moved her hands from his back to his front, sliding them up his chest, to his neck. She removed the band from his hair, and tangled her hands in it, letting the silky strands caress her fingers.

Stretching upward and winding her hands around his neck, she pressed the full length of her body against him.

This time, he moaned.

His mouth moved to her neck. His hands went back to her waist, his grip firm as he pulled her toward him, rubbing his hips against hers, his cock kissing her pussy.

"Oh, yes," she breathed, pressing her hips forward, tilting them upward, then downward.

The air hissed from him. His grip tightened, holding her still.

"If you want to keep our deal," he rasped against her neck, "then you have about five seconds to move away from me."

Alyssa opened her eyes, becoming aware of her mouth against Tony's neck, her hands fisted in his hair, her breasts flattened against his chest, her hips pressed as close as she could get them to his.

She was even standing on tiptoe for better access.

So much for showing restraint. It was pretty bad when the guy had to tell you to stop. Alyssa's face felt warm.

She slid her body down his.

He cursed, his hands tightening on her waist.

"Oh. Right. The deal." She took a deep breath. It was shaky. Staring at his neck, she straightened the collar that she had wrinkled. Probably when she had clutched it in her hands to pull him down to her. My God, he must think she was . . . desperate.

She was desperate. For his touch. For his taste.

"Sorry. I kind of forgot about the deal for a minute. Despite my actions, I do want to stick to it. I—"

"Two seconds." His voice was strained.

"Oh." Alyssa pulled back, out of his arms. "Well, then. I'll just take this dress and go get ready."

She yanked the dress from the floor, unaware that it had fallen, and scampered past him, heading for the bathroom.

"Alyssa."

She paused and turned, forcing herself to look at him.

His hair hung to his shoulders, mussed as if a woman had ran her hands through it. His lips looked pinker, as if a woman had kissed him repeatedly, giving him all the passion that had lain sleeping inside of her—passion that she hadn't thought about in a while. His clothing looked rumpled, as if a woman had pulled and tugged at it, desperate to get him naked and feel his flesh against hers.

Alyssa had done all of that—and wanted to do more.

She met his gaze.

His eyes were narrowed. "I only stopped because of you. Your job. I can't promise to next time."

With that, he turned and exited the bedroom.

5

Tony stood in front of the bar in Giovanni's home office, watching the man's lips move, but paying little attention. Instead, he was thinking of Alyssa's lips. How they'd parted almost instantly under his, just as eager to let him explore as he'd been to explore. How soft and smooth they'd been, moving in sync with his, giving one minute, demanding the next.

And her body, pressed against his, urging him to take her . . .

His cock stirred.

He'd wanted to fuck her. He couldn't remember wanting a woman so badly before.

As such, his parting words had been a half-lie. True, he couldn't promise that he'd stop next time. But the real truth was, he wasn't even going to try.

In a way, it was her fault—if she hadn't given him such a passionate response to his kiss, he'd let her hide behind that contract. But now . . . Hell, there was no way he was turning down the opportunity to see all that passion unleashed.

If only he didn't have this business with Giovanni to attend to.

Another first, when had some woman been more interesting than business? That thought caused him to frown. He pushed it from his mind and forced himself to pay attention to Giovanni.

". . . which is why Strands holds a special place in my heart . . ." said Giovanni.

Bullshit, thought Tony. Giovanni Maffucci's ego resided where his heart should've been.

". . . so I want a buyer willing to carry on the tradition . . ."

Which really meant he wanted a sucker to keep the club as is, which included preservation of the Maffucci shrine—complete with a wax figure of Giovanni behind glass—smack dab in the entrance to the club.

When Strands was his, Tony was considering having a bonfire at the grand opening, letting guests feed items of memorabilia into the flames.

Personally, Tony didn't like Giovanni. Giovanni screwed employees—literally and figuratively, implemented poor customer service, skimmed money by inflating expenses, and never reinvested the profits to improve the business. And those were his better qualities. It was a wonder that Strands was still showing a profit.

Profit was all that Tony cared about. Giovanni's sleaze factor was his own problem. Business was business.

As Giovanni gazed out the window toward the pool and droned on with feigned nostalgia, Tony's mind drifted back to Alyssa—correction: Lissy.

He smiled at the memory of her horrified expression when he'd come up with their nicknames. And her near panic when she saw the clothes he'd bought for her to wear. That had been a switch—most of the women he knew would've hid their distaste, so intent on becoming the first Mrs. Brooks, no attire would have been unacceptable. Of course, Alyssa wasn't campaigning for a permanent position in his life.

Maybe that was her appeal. Well, that and the fact that she was a far cry from his usual dates—women who were artificially perfected, blonde-by-the-bottle, salon-pampered, botox-enhanced, and breast-augmented. Not that they were his type, either. They just seemed to be the ones he met in the entertainment business. The plastic women, who strove so hard for perfection, that they were almost untouchable—physically and emotionally.

The emotional part didn't bother him, as he had no desire—or time—for emotional involvement. But the physical part eventually became a showstopper. Perfection didn't mix well with sex that was hot, sweaty, and messy.

But hot, sweaty, and messy sex seemed like it would mix well with Lissy.

Because she oozed naturalness. Sun-kissed hair that he could weave his hands through. Smooth, makeup-free skin he could touch and nibble. Round, plump, real breasts that would fill his hands, that he could cover with licks and kisses, that he could caress and squeeze, sending lust crashing through both of them.

And those rosy, pouty lips. God, one quick taste of them had him fantasizing about feeling them on his skin, moving from his mouth and down his neck, her tongue swirling against his flesh, as she moved lower. To his chest, over his stomach . . .

His pants felt tight.

And, what surprised him was that he actually enjoyed talking to her. Not that they'd done more than sparred about this silly date-for-hire situation. But she'd made it . . . enjoyable.

Now, there was a word that hadn't been used in a sentence with his name in it for a very long time. No time. Business took up most of his time and, while he enjoyed it, it was a different type of enjoyment. Not that he was complaining. He hadn't even given it much thought until now.

Until Alyssa.

But of course, that was what she did for a living—making men feel at ease, making sure they enjoyed their . . ."date." He smiled. Scratch the word "men" and make it "man." He was her first. She was making sure that he enjoyed his date.

His smile faded and he frowned.

Is that what she'd been doing upstairs, pretending so that his "date" would be enjoyable?

No, she couldn't be. She'd have to be one hell of an actress—

A movement in the hallway outside the door drew his gaze. Unaware that she was being observed, Alyssa chewed her lower lip as she pulled—or tried to pull—the dress down to cover more of her thighs. She looked down the front of her dress and pulled up, attempting to cover her chest, but only succeeding in shortening its length.

Tony's cock lengthened.

Alyssa sighed, repeated the pulling-over-the-hip action, then cupped her breasts—

Tony swallowed. Hard.

—and pushed upward, then adjusted the drape of the slinky material. She took a deep breath that, to his cock's delight, pushed the fleshy globes tight against the fabric, revealing the slight outline of her nipples.

Feeling as if all the oxygen had been sucked from the room, Tony gulped in air.

Alyssa looked up. Surprise flitted across her face.

Tony smiled—what he hoped was a casual, hey-baby-you-look-good smile, not the leering, I'll-give-anything-to-be-inside-you smile he was feeling.

Alyssa blushed, confirming he'd given her the casual smile. Squaring her shoulders, she took another deep breath.

Like a trained lab rat, Tony's eyes once again dropped to her chest, obsessed by the nipples he suddenly prayed would pop out of the dress. When she exhaled, his gaze returned to her face.

She smiled. A sultry I'll-do-anything-to-be-with-you smile.

Stunned, the breath caught in his chest.

He watched her take small, bouncy steps into the room, her eyes never leaving his, the smile never leaving her face.

"Tonykins," she squealed.

He felt his mouth drop open.

"There you are. I thought I'd never find you. I got lost coming down the stairs, and there were all these hallways and doors . . ." She giggled and jiggled up to him. "But now I'm . . . here." She stood on tiptoe, her breasts pressing into his forearm.

Heat rushed to his groin.

He'd barely remembered to close his mouth when she pressed her lips against his. The softness of her lips, the minty scent of her toothpaste, coupled with her hot body pressed the length of his caused an instinctive craving to deepen the kiss. Just as he moved his lips against hers, she moved away.

"Oh . . . this handsome man must be Mr. Maffucci," she purred, sticking out a limp hand—when did she paint her nails hot pink? "So *very* nice to meet you."

Tony watched in amazement as Giovanni, who'd turned from the window when she'd flounced in, straightened and sucked in his gut. He took her hand in his, bringing it to his fleshy lips.

"You must be Alyssa. An unusual name but it sounds familiar." He paused for a minute, frowning.

Did Alyssa stiffen?

Giovanni's frown faded and he smiled—leered—and continued. "Tony neglected to mention how . . ." his gaze slithered over her body, lingering on her breasts. He licked his fleshy lips. ". . . charming you were."

Tony frowned.

Alyssa giggled. Again. "Oh, he always forgets to tell people that, don't you, baby?" She swatted his arm playfully.

Giovanni's gaze was still riveted to her breasts.

Tony's lips tightened.

He slid his arm around her waist and pulled her to him, pressing a light kiss on her forehead. "That's because I don't want to share you, Lissy." His voice had an edge he didn't mean it to.

Giovanni chuckled. "And well you shouldn't, my man."

Alyssa turned to Tony, her mouth a moue of surprise. "Baby, are you jealous?"

Tony felt his face grow warm. Of course he wasn't jealous. He never—

She took his cheeks between her thumb and forefinger, pinching and jiggling them like one did an infant. "Oh, Tonykins," she said in baby talk, "you know I *wone-wee* want you."

Tony's face felt hot. No one had ever tweaked his cheeks and treated him like a baby, not even when he *was* a baby.

Giovanni laughed.

Alyssa smiled, slid her arm around his waist, pressed her body against his, and turned to Giovanni. "Were you boys discussing that business stuff?" She waved her hand dismissively before resting it on Tony's chest.

"Yes, as a matter of fact, we were," said Giovanni.

Alyssa fidgeted against him, her pussy rubbing against his thigh, while her fingers played with the button on his shirt. Tony gritted his teeth and placed his hand over hers, stopping their motion.

She looked up at him, pouting. "I hope you're done, Tonykins. You promised not to talk about boring stuff. You said we were going to have fun."

Keeping the lust careening through his body in check, he bent his knee slightly and rubbed his thigh lightly between her legs.

This time, her moue of surprise was real. As was her gasp.

He smiled down at her. "Baby, we are going to have fun. I promise."

"No time like the present," said Giovanni, oblivious to Tony's double entendre.

Alyssa wasn't. She blushed and quickly looked away, turning her attention to their host.

Satisfaction zinged through Tony. One point for the home team. Finally.

"Tony, why don't you make us fresh drinks. And I'm sure Lissy is thirsty."

"Oh, yes." She nodded eagerly, her blond hair brushing her shoulders.

Giovanni looked just as eager as he took her hands and led her to the couch.

She sat.

Giovanni sat next to her. Too close.

Tony clenched his jaw, pivoted and went to the bar. "What would you like, Lissy?"

She waved at him dismissively, her rapt gaze upon Giovanni. "The usual."

Barely paying attention to their conversation, he splashed whatever liquor his hands touched into a glass, then made a gin and tonic for Giovanni. In record time, he carried the glasses to the couch and sat next to Alyssa.

He put his arm around her shoulder and pulled her to him.

She took a sip, then coughed and sputtered, tears streaming down her face. "Wow," she said, glaring at him. "That's really good, Tonykins."

He grinned, feeling back in the game, and stroked her cheek with the back of his finger. "Only the best for you, baby."

"Thank you," she said sweetly. She stuck her tongue out at him before turning back to Giovanni. "I like a drink with a little . . . kick." She took another sip for show. Though her eyes watered, she didn't cough. She set the glass down. To Tony, it looked like with relief.

Tony sat back, suddenly enjoying himself.

"So tell me, Lissy, what do you do for a living?"

Tony took a sip, curious to hear what creative answer she was going to come up with.

"I'm a . . . gymnast."

Tony choked.

She turned to him, resting her hand on his thigh, drawing little circles with her forefinger against the fabric, faux concern plastered on her face. "Tonykins, are you okay?"

His cock woke up. He nodded, catching his breath.

She swung back around, before pressing hard against his leg, using his thigh for leverage to stand. "Wanna see some of my moves?"

"Yes!" said Giovanni.

"No!" said Tony.

Tony watched Alyssa bounce away from them. The dress hugged her thighs and cupped her ass. With each step, the exaggerated sway of her hips threatened to pull the tight material upward, giving a tantalizing glimpse of an ass cheek.

She stopped and turned toward them. She took a bow, revealing a cock-hardening amount of breast and cleavage.

Giovanni inhaled sharply.

Alyssa turned to the side and raised her hands over her head.

Tony sprang from the couch.

"I learned to do the splits when I was five—"

He reached her side and grabbed her arm. "You are not going to do the splits," he ground out.

He led her back to the couch and pulled her down, this time onto his lap where he could make sure she didn't go anywhere.

"I'm wearing a dress, silly—I wasn't going to do the splits." Her tone was huffy. "I was going to do a handstand."

Giovanni laughed.

Alyssa pouted. "You didn't have to be such a pitty poo, Tonykins."

"I agree, pitty poo Tonykins," said Giovanni, chortling.

Alyssa squirmed and turned excitedly to Giovanni, "Your house is beautiful. Tell me all about it."

Giovanni puffed up and began telling about the rooms in loving detail. Since there was at least 6,000 square feet of living space, Tony figured the conversation was going to take a long time. Especially with Alyssa asking him questions and squealing and squirming with delight.

Alyssa wiggled again and Tony gritted his teeth, the hand that had been lightly stroking her shoulder, tightening, giving her the subtle hint to stop.

She stopped, thankfully getting the hint.

His head hurt. And he was so aroused, his balls hurt. This evening was not going as planned. He hadn't thought he'd have to sit around and watch Giovanni practically drool over Alyssa all night. Where the hell was his girlfriend?

Baby, are you jealous? Alyssa had chirped.

Hell, no. That was ridiculous. He just wanted this mind-numbing conversation to end.

Alyssa laughed at something Giovanni said and rubbed her ass against his crotch.

Desire stabbed his groin.

His head throbbed.

He leaned forward and whispered in her ear, "Do that one more time and I will send Giovanni on some errand and fuck you right here on this couch."

He kissed the back of her neck.

She stilled, not moving a muscle while Giovanni droned on.

Tony forced his jaw to relax. Giovanni was getting on his last nerve. With every word that came out of his mouth, Tony's dislike for him grew. He was pompous, selfish, and an egomaniac. Tony'd much rather be sequestered with Alyssa upstairs, in bed—

Bed.

For the first time in over thirty minutes, Tony smiled. She'd called it a sultan's bed. Actually, it did resemble one. He wondered if there were any feathers in any of the drawers. If so, he'd lay Alyssa, completely naked, on the bed and make her lie still while he ran the feather down her body, over her neck, and across her shoulders, drawing circles on her breasts before lightly tickling her nipples. She'd gasp and arch, wanting more. Begging him to take her in his mouth, to—

"Shall we head to dinner?" asked Giovanni, interrupting Tony's fantasy.

"Yes!" he said.

"Yes, I'm famished!" said Alyssa.

Giovanni smiled for the hundredth time at Alyssa. "Good. I want you to meet Bimbi. I'm sure the two of you will have a lot to talk about."

Alyssa clapped her hands together lightly. "Oh, that sounds like fun."

As Giovanni led them from the room, Alyssa turned to Tony. Laughter sparkled in her eyes, her cheeks were flushed, and she looked thoroughly kissable.

He resisted the urge to lean down and make her face burn with a different kind of heat, to—

"Do you think 'Bimbi' stands for 'bimbo'?" she whispered.

"Speaking of bimbos, maybe you should tone down the ditzy act a bit."

"Oh, no," she said, surprise rippling through her tone.

190

"Giovanni likes it. Your deal is in the bag. What—you don't think it's working?"

Hell, yeah, it was working. Too well. Giovanni looked about two steps away from making Alyssa part of the deal.

So what's the problem? If that's what it takes . . . Business is business, right?

6

Standing in the middle of the bathroom in Giovanni's pool house, Alyssa massaged her temples with the pads of her fingers. Her head was killing her. The strain of fawning all over Tony, of constantly sidling up to him, of feeling the muscles of his arm flex against her or the brush of his leg against her hip—

God, that was nothing compared to sitting on Tony's lap in Giovanni's office. *That* had been torture. Every time she'd moved, his cock was there, pressing against her ass, a constant reminder of what she wanted but couldn't have. And he kept moving, shifting his hips, pressing his cock closer, which caused her to move, to try to get comfortable, to try to move away.

Do that one more time and I will send Giovanni on some errand and fuck you right here on this couch.

His words, combined with the accompanying agonized growl, had almost brought her to orgasm. If he had kissed the back of her neck for just a second longer, she would've.

Then there was the agony of dinner, where Tony kept his hand on her thigh, massaging and caressing her under the table. What was up with that? Giovanni couldn't even see Tony's hand, so it couldn't have been for his sake. Unless Tony had wanted to keep Alyssa's face permanently flushed, thereby giving the appearance of continual arousal.

Appearances be damned. It was reality. Alyssa was aroused, more aroused than she could remember being in months.

Well, it didn't take much to top that record, for she hadn't been aroused *at all* in months.

Whatever.

Alyssa opened her eyes and walked to the sink. She stared at her face in the mirror. It was still flushed, still mirroring her lust.

She turned on the cold water, cupped her hands under the stream, and splashed water on her face. Again and again, then used the fluffy white hand towel to pat her skin dry.

She didn't feel any better. She still felt tense and her head still ached.

The constant state of arousal was the cause of her tension, while the strain of being bubbly and perky and clueless had given her a headache. Or maybe it was the other way around. Or maybe both were caused by horniness.

Oh, what did it matter? What mattered was that her body and her mind were both tied in knots and she was strung as taut as a rubber band.

The next time she heard another dumb blonde joke, she was going to be doubly outraged—not only because she did not fit the cliché, but also because those who did deserved respect. Being ditzy was damn hard work.

Speaking of work, it was time she got back to it.

Alyssa turned to the floor-length mirror on the door for one last look at the bathing suit Tony had bought for her. Eighty percent of her breasts spilled out of the miniscule triangles designed to cover little more than her nipples. And the bikini bottom ... well, if she hadn't had a Brazilian wax done two days ago, things could've been quite ugly. Literally. The triangle that covered her pussy was only slightly wider and longer than the ones that failed to cover her chest.

She sighed.

Surely, being dressed like a stripper must be against some rule in Shannon's "corporate" escort handbook.

She wouldn't have thought it possible for the leopard skin patterned bathing suit to look sluttier on than it had spread across the bed.

Bed.

As in, the piece of furniture that she and Tony would find themselves lying atop in a handful of hours.

God.

How was she going to get through the night without ... sinning—which would land her both in heaven, because of the heights to which Tony took her body, and in breach of contract, because she'd signed away the right for Tony to take her to heaven.

It made her head spin.

Letting out another deep sigh, Alyssa reached for the filmy wrap and tied it around her hips. Despite its see-through nature, she felt less naked. With one last look, she exited the bathroom, returned to the torch-lit pool, and—

Stopped dead in her tracks.

Hyperventilation was added as ailment number five to her current list, preceded only by number four, want; number three, desire; number two, need; and number one, lust.

The source of ailment numbers one through five reclined on a lounge chair, clad only in a Speedo-type bathing suit. Unable to stop herself, Alyssa let her gaze wander hungrily over Tony's tanned legs, lingering on his muscular thighs and the muscle-of-choice, hidden behind the black Lycra, before moving higher over his toned abs and honed pecs.

God, how could it be possible for a man to *be* mouth-watering?

Struggling to mask her thoughts, she raised her gaze to his face only to discover that Tony had been taking a journey of his own. His gaze roved her body, lingering on the same spots that'd intrigued her when exploring his body. His eyes stroked her legs . . . caressed her thighs . . . penetrated the sheerness of her wrap and stroked her pussy, generating heat . . . circled her waist like a lasso, pulling her toward him . . . swept across her breasts, making her nipples peak and strain toward him . . . and finally, landed on her face.

His eyes smoldered.

"Alyssa, come join us," said Giovanni.

Her gaze flickered to him, taking note of Bimbi sprawled on a chair pulled close to his, her bathing suit equally as nonexistent as Alyssa's.

"Lissy, come join *me*," Tony said, drawing her attention back to him. His voice seduced, tangling with the invisible rope still looped around her waist, pulling her toward him.

Tony patted his chair.

Her gaze dropped to the spot he indicated, directly in front of his hips, before zooming in on the bulge in his trunks that hadn't been there seconds before.

If she sat in front of him, she'd feel his cock against her ass—again—and she'd lose the remnants of pride that she was hanging onto with her pinky and turn into him and kiss the lips that she'd been fantasizing about all evening, and roll on top of him, grinding her hips against his, desperate to feel him inside her.

Right in front of Bimbi and Giovanni.

Not that Giovanni would mind. He'd probably whip out his camcorder and film it for one of his "gentlemen's" clubs.

She shuddered. The night had shown her that Giovanni was a bigger sleaze than she'd imagined. Thank God Bimbi had arrived to take Giovanni's attention off Alyssa.

Or maybe she wasn't thankful. Because dealing with her revulsion to Giovanni was a thousand times easier than dealing with her attraction to Tony.

Nope. There was no way she was going over there to Tony's cock—er, chair. Just as there was no way she was going to be able to keep her no-sex promise to Shannon.

But she should at least give it one last try, shouldn't she?

Her panicked gaze returned to Tony's. His eyes were hooded, his lips curled in a slight smile that said he could see the battle going on inside her. He picked up a drink from the table beside the chair and held it out to her while, once again, patting the place in front of him with the other.

Getting drunk was the last thing she needed. What she needed was strength.

She giggled. "I want to swim first, Tonykins." Her giggle sounded like a cackle. Her voice sounded shrill. But she didn't care. Turning, she stripped off her wrap and dove into the pool.

He body sliced through the water. The water closed over her head, blocking out all sound, preventing her from hearing any response Tony might've made. Facedown, coming up for air every fifth or sixth stroke, she made her way to one end of the pool, turned, and swam to the opposite end. Once . . . twice . . . by the third time, she felt sufficiently winded and decided to slow down. When she reached the deep end, she grabbed hold of the edge and came to a sputtering stop.

"We thought maybe you were training for the Olympics," said Giovanni with a laugh from the poolside behind her.

She forced another giggle, unable to think of a brainless rejoinder, and wiped the water out of her eyes with one hand.

She'd hoped that the laps would help her work off some of her sexual tension, which still buzzed through her.

A loud splash, followed by the sound of strokes, caused her to turn her head in time to see Tony's body cut gracefully through the water, heading in the opposite direction.

Alyssa turned her body around so that her shoulder blades rested against the edge of the pool, stretching her arms along the ledge to hold herself afloat. She watched Tony turn, push off against the side of the pool and glide almost soundlessly toward her.

His muscles rippled with each stroke.

Her body throbbed with each stroke.

He stopped in front of her, treading water. His hair had come loose from the band holding it back and it hung in his face, covering his eyes. He ducked underwater, held his head back, and once again bobbed to the surface.

"Hi," he said, unsmiling.

"Hi," she said, breathless. Though more from his nearness than from the half dozen laps she'd just rushed through.

"You weren't thirsty, I take it."

"Thirsty?"

"The drink."

"Oh . . ." Her mind flashed back on the delicious visual—his hard cock straining against the tight material—that had sent her scurrying to the pool. *No, I was—am—hungry. Starving for a taste of you.* "No . . . I . . . You . . . "

He was too close. His breath blew all thoughts out of her mind, while flooding her body with need—the need to press closer.

She pressed her body back against the tiled wall.

He stopped treading water and kept himself afloat by holding on to the ledge on either side of her head. He dipped a leg between hers, his knee brushing her inner thigh. Alyssa clasped her legs together, preventing his leg from going higher.

She gasped. "Tony, this is not supposed to happen." She kept her voice low so Giovanni and Bimbi couldn't hear. Not that they could anyway, given they were at least thirty feet away.

"You're a beautiful woman. I'm a mere man."

Oh, God. A flesh-and-blood Roman god had just called her beautiful.

Her heart melted, her lips curved into a smile.

"What did you expect, coming out here almost naked?"

Her smile evaporated. "You bought this suit!"

"Doesn't change the fact that you're nearly naked." His fingertips caressed the sensitive skin of her inner arm.

His leg moved upward, despite the feeble attempt of her thighs to stop him, and nestled against her crotch. "The faint outline of your pussy lips made my cock hard."

She exhaled noisily.

He slid his hand fractionally and his fingers brushed the sides of her breasts.

She inhaled sharply.

He leaned forward, and spoke near her ear. "I could see your nipples harden when you saw my cock." His tongue flicked her earlobe. "You've been teasing me all night, Alyssa."

"You wanted me to tease you." Her voice cracked.

"I wanted you to adore me."

"How can I adore you without teasing you?"

"You should've asked that question a lot earlier."

No sex. No sex. No sex.

"Tony." Her voice pleaded. "I was just trying to do my job."

"You excel at your job. Your giggle reminded me of the sound a woman makes during sex. When she's being pleasured beyond her wildest dreams."

Oh, man, she wanted to be pleasured beyond her wettest, wildest, most graphic dreams.

"And your brainless act had Giovanni panting after you . . ." He nibbled her earlobe.

She shivered.

"I was jealous."

She gasped. "You were?"

His mouth moved to the corner of hers. His chest rubbed against hers. "I really would have fucked you there. You know that, don't you?"

"N-no."

"Do you know I'm going to fuck you now?"

His words made her lightheaded, as the blood rushed from her head and swelled her pussy lips. Desperation caused her to try a different approach. "But you don't like brainless women!"

"You've taught me to appreciate their appeal."

"But The Perfect Date code of ethics . . ." Her ace card. Her only hope of stopping him. "I signed it. Sex could cost me my job." Oh. Right. She didn't care if she had a job. "I mean, it could cost Shannon her business."

"I won't tell if you don't." His voice was like honey. His tongue traced her lips. "Kiss me, Alyssa."

She parted her lips to say . . . Yes . . . No . . . Ah, hell, she didn't know what she'd been going to say.

He bit her lip lightly. His thigh brushed against her thigh. Sensation pummeled her body.

She groaned.

"Alyssa."

"Yes?" she asked, not sure if she said the word out loud.

His tongue dipped between her lips. "Kiss me. Like you did before."

Oh, God, yes, kiss him, Alyssa!

Sorry, Shannon. I tried.

Alyssa moaned softly—a moan of surrender—and slanted her head. She moved her lips over his, sneaking her tongue inside his mouth, stealing a taste of rum mixed with need, lust mixed with man. She pressed forward, forcing the kiss deeper, demanding his passion.

A groan rumbled beneath his ribs. Pressing forward, he satisfied her demand, meeting her tongue thrust for thrust, taste for taste. Giving her his passion, while taking hers.

She wanted more than a kiss. More than the tease of his body brushing hers, the water trying to separate them.

Alyssa slid her foot up his leg.

His gasp filled her mouth.

She slid her foot down his leg.

He pressed his hips forward.

Her gasp filled his mouth.

"Wrap your legs around me." Pain underlined his words.

Sharing his pain, Alyssa wrapped her legs around his hips—and nearly fainted. His cock grazed her pussy, so close, so potent, despite the layers of stretchy fabric separating them.

She tightened her legs, pulling him closer. She removed her arms from the ledge and wrapped them around his neck. Her chest flattened against his, her pussy rubbed against his cock.

Tony moaned softly.

Giovanni yelled from the poolside, "Get a hotel room."

Bimbi tittered.

Alyssa opened her eyes, yanked from the world of the senses. Lust warred with . . . embarrassment.

Tony's cock pulsed against her lower lips.

Her nipples throbbed against his chest.

God, if Giovanni hadn't interrupted them, she would've fucked Tony right in front of his eyes. And what made things even worse was the fact that the lust still raging through her veins made her want to fuck Tony, regardless of who might be watching.

"We're thinking about it," said Tony, not taking his eyes off of her.

Giovanni laughed.

Tony didn't.

Alyssa slid her legs down Tony's body, intending to move away.

"Don't move," Tony said, removing one hand from the ledge to grab her leg and stop its slide.

"Tony, I don't think we—"

"Don't think." His head dropped to her neck, suckling. His fingers glided to her inner thigh, and slid underneath her suit, seeking . . .

"Oh—" she breathed.

. . . finding . . .

She gripped his neck, clutching him as if he were a lifesaver. Which, maybe he was, since he was now the only thing keeping her afloat.

His finger sped against her clit, making the little nub as rigid as the cock she felt through his trunks, which was caressing her thigh.

She struggled to remain still, for if she didn't grind her hips in time to his finger, urging him faster and harder, no one would know that Tony was finger banging her in the water, that she was two seconds from coming, that—

"Touch me," he rasped in her ear.

Still dazed by Tony's strokes, she removed one arm from his neck, trailing it down his body, to his trunks. She slipped her hand inside, brushing the crinkly hair with her fingertips as they made their way to his cock.

Tony nipped her neck with his teeth.

His finger sped up, sending her higher.

She found her rhythm, circling his hardness, stroking his cock.

"Put me inside you."

Sanity made a brief appearance. "Not here. They'll know."

"You think they don't already know?"

His finger slipped into her pussy, then moved back to her clit. Pussy . . . clit . . . pussy . . . clit.

"You think they care? They've got business of their own."

Tony's back was to the poolside couple but Alyssa's wasn't. She raised her eyes and looked.

"Do you care, Alyssa? Are you going to tell me to stop?"

Her eyes fluttered closed, his words making her dizzy, while his finger made her body shake.

"No . . . "

"No, what?"

She opened her eyes, fighting Tony's spell for the briefest of seconds. She needed to know . . .

Sure enough, Giovanni and Bimbi weren't paying attention to her and Tony. In fact, they were about to get their own little orgy started, judging by the lip-lock Bimbi had him in.

Not that it mattered anymore. "No, I don't care."

Tony's probing fingers jerked her attention back to him.

"No, I don't want you to stop."

Her nails dug into his shoulders as the tension within her pooled in her pussy, swirling and roiling and . . .

She tried to hold back.

It was too much to hold back.

All the teasing and taunting, touching and caressing, had taken its toll. Tony's touch released the chaos churning inside her, causing it to explode outward, causing her body to tremble and quiver.

She managed to hold back the scream that lodged in her throat.

She managed to hold onto Tony, to not become the first woman to drown while coming.

God, that was great. Most probably the best—

"Alyssa?"

Alyssa blinked, coming back to reality for the second time in two minutes. She focused on Tony, noting the agonized expression on his face.

"Put me inside you."

Oh. Right. His needs. Give a girl a mind-blowing orgasm and, well, there goes her mind.

She lifted her legs higher, wrapping them around his hips, and positioned his cock near her pussy.

His fingers pulled her bikini bottoms to the side.

She put him at her entrance.

He jerked, straining to get closer.

And just like that, his cock turned his need into hers. Digging the heels of her feet into his ass, she pulled her hips forward slightly, letting him in an inch.

He cursed.

She gasped and buried him inside her another inch.

His hand left her, joining his other hand on the ledge. He tried to pump his hips forward, but had nothing to ground his legs against, so her back touched the edge of the pool, before the water carried them a few inches away.

Wow. Tony was helpless. While he had nothing to use as leverage and had to keep both hands—or at least one—on the ledge to keep them from drowning, her hands and legs were free. He was dependent on her for his satisfaction.

How cool was that?

This realization ratcheted her arousal up another ten degrees.

"Tony?"

"What."

Gee, that sure sounded painful.

"You want to be inside me . . . like . . . this . . . ?" Using her heels, Alyssa pulled her hips all the way forward. A moan slipped from her throat.

"Oh, God." The words were a tortured moan from his throat.

Alyssa struggled to keep her desire in check, to focus on him. She clutched his shoulder with one hand to keep herself anchored, then grabbed his hip with the other. Pushing with the hand on his hip, she propelled her hips backward, away from him.

His cock slid halfway out of her pussy.

Pulling with her hand and her legs, still wrapped around his hips, she drew his cock back in her pussy.

"Is this what you had in mind, Tony?"

"Yes!"

She pushed him out of her, then pulled him back in.

"Faster."

She went faster. The water churned around them, disturbed by her actions, splashing up, getting in her eyes.

She closed her eyes, the turbulence in the water matching the turbulence inside her.

They made no effort to be quiet.

He called her name.

She cried out.

His breathing was ragged.

Her breathing was loud.

She was on the edge, the point where every nerve and cell seemed to be as one, motionless and waiting for the sensation roiling through her body to explode and send her insides into a flurry of motion.

All activity beyond what was being done to her body ceased to have meaning. At this moment, Tony's cock stroking her pussy was the only thing that mattered to her.

He grunted. He bit her shoulder. He moaned her name.

All of which broke the dam within her body, releasing the need struggling to get free.

Alyssa let go of Tony's hip and clutched his neck with both hands, holding on tight, pressing him as close as possible to her, needing to feel his spasms both inside and against her body.

Tony buried his head in the curve of her neck as his body surrendered to his release.

Alyssa listened to his breathing and the silence around them. Giovanni and Bimbi had left. The water was still.

Alyssa relaxed.

Once his body felt relaxed, she unwound her arms from Tony's neck and separated their bodies while simultaneously reaching behind her for the ledge.

She kissed his forehead.

He kissed her lips.

Inching to her right, Tony flattened his palms against the ledge and used his arms to push. He propelled his torso out of the water, then threw his leg onto the side of the pool, and stood.

Turning, he reached down, took Alyssa's hand, and pulled her out of the water.

Still holding onto her, he led her to the lounge chair and picked up her wrap and two towels. He wrapped one around her and tucked the other over his hips.

This time, he kissed her on her forehead and said, "Come on."

"Where are we going?"

He grinned and winked at her. "To bed."

7

Standing in front of the bed, Alyssa toweled her hair dry. Her skin felt clean. Her body felt energized—from the shower, certainly. From the knowledge of what was in store for her, most definitely.

The sound of drawers opening and closing drew her gaze to Tony.

"What are you looking for?"

He turned from the nightstand and grinned at her.

"Feathers."

"Feathers?"

"Yeah. While you were giving me that lap dance in Giovanni's office, I fantasized about spreading you naked on the bed, stroking your body with feathers, teasing you—"

Her body hummed from the visual. "Let me help you look." Her voice was a croak.

Tony laughed.

Both were disappointed when every drawer had been opened and every corner had been searched. No feathers.

Alyssa walked over to the bed, going to one set of curtains then the other, removing the ropes.

Ropes in hand, she walked over to Tony, who stood at the foot of the bed. "Great minds think alike," she said, rubbing the rope along his arms.

"How's that?"

"Well, while you were imaging feather torture, I was imagining tying you up with this rope and teasing you like this . . ." She ran her tongue over his chest, ending with his nipples.

They hardened.

". . . And this . . ." She wrapped her hand around his cock.

His cock hardened.

Tony wrapped his hands around her hand. "I don't do ropes." His voice was hoarse.

Her voice teased. "Is the mighty Tony Brooks afraid of a little brainless gal like me?"

"Yes," he said. He took her hands in his and forced her backward until her legs butted up against the bed. Slipping the rope from her hands, he pushed her.

She toppled onto the bed.

Tony climbed on top of her, straddling her hips. "Plus, it's my turn."

"Your turn for what?"

"To have you helpless. Like you had me in the pool."

He pulled her hand toward the headboard.

She pulled her hand back. "But you could get away if you wanted."

"The knots will be loose so you can slip out of them if you want. But I hope you won't."

Tony tied one arm, then the next.

Alyssa shivered. "I feel silly. Like a pig ready for roasting." Her laugh was nervous.

Tony parted the towel and ran his hands over her—down

her breasts, stomach, hips and back up.

The touch stoked a familiar fire.

"You don't look silly." His voice was husky.

Leaning down, he flicked his tongue along her neck and down to her breasts. "But you are definitely a feast."

His mouth nibbled her stomach. His tongue snuck into her navel.

The wetness thrilled her.

He drew back, his eyes blazing. "I really was jealous, you know. Of Giovanni's eyes on you. Of the thoughts running through his mind, thoughts identical to mine."

His words thrilled her.

"I wanted you to be only with me." He undid the towel around his waist, raised off her to pull it off, and flung it onto the floor before resuming his position.

His cock stroked her stomach.

She pulled on the ropes.

"Did I make your first time memorable?"

"Yes. So much so that . . . my first time is going to be my last time." Her attempt to sound playful failed.

"This is the last time?" Tension threaded his voice.

"My last time at The Perfect Match."

Tony smiled and resumed his teasing. He moved his hips down, letting his cock rest against her cleft. "I like that answer because I'd like to see you again. When we get home. Not as a Perfect Date."

He put his cock near the entrance to her pussy.

She jutted her hips.

He laughed.

Before she surrendered to his pull, begged for her release, there was one question she had to ask. "Why did you hire a date, when you could've had any woman you wanted?"

Tony stilled. "Because an escort is bound by a confidentiality agreement. Unlike a 'real date'—like the last woman, who talked to an online columnist."

Alyssa tensed and her arousal evaporated. He was talking about Chantelle. He was talking about her. He was talking about her article, "Chantelle Dubois Flies to France for a Yummy Dessert."

"Relax," whispered Tony. He pressed a fingertip against her lips. "No more questions. No more talking. Only feeling."

And as Tony tasted her breasts, words fled from her mind. As he gripped her hips, she forgot how to talk. As he thrust his cock inside of her, she felt only him. His touch, his body.

She thrust her hips, meeting him stroke for stroke.

She yanked on the ropes, straining to get closer, desperate to feel more of him.

He gave and withheld, entered her and withdrew.

Mindless gibberish flew from her lips.

Guttural grunts rumbled in his throat.

As her need merged with his, as her soul sought his, as her orgasm mated with his, her passion washed away the discomfort created by his words.

8

Alyssa gripped the railing as she walked down the stairs in her three-inch heels. Thank God today was the last day of this charade. Either her mind or her neck was going to snap.

She breathed a sigh of relief as she reached the bottom of the stairs. Only twenty more steps to the dining room and then she could hang onto Tony's arm, thereby increasing her odds of making it home alive.

Home.

Tony had said he wanted to see her once they were back home, back to their real lives. A real date, he'd said. One that involved the use of her brain and flat-heeled shoes and a baseball cap, after which they'd engage in a round of bedroom gymnastics, her being a "gymnast" and all.

She smiled.

Now there was an outing to make the God-awful jiggle she had to put into her Ditzy Girl step real. Her mind zipped back to their recent sex and her face warmed. She never would've guessed that she'd like being trussed and tied, that giving into the feeling of being powerless could heighten her orgasm.

She now knew firsthand what Tony must've experienced in the pool, why his climax had been so fast.

Pushing thoughts of sex from her mind, she sighed. One more act and she was through. After adjusting her dress for the tenth useless time, she peeked into the dining room. A buffet was spread out on the side table but no one was there.

She frowned.

Tony had said 11:30, but maybe his meeting with Giovanni was running late.

Great. That meant she'd have to go to the office, which meant thirty more steps. Maybe she should just take off the damn shoes.

No. It was too much work getting them back on. Taking a deep breath and using the wall for support, she made her way down the hall, careful not to get her toothpick heels caught in the plush carpet.

Outside of the door to Giovanni's office, she paused and peeked inside. The two men were at Giovanni's desk, staring at his computer screen. Plastering a big smile on her face, Alyssa knocked and pushed the door open. "Heeellllooooo," she said in a singsong voice.

Which would have been the perfect greeting had the two men been in a singsong mood. Instead, two hostile faces turned her way. Giovanni looked like he'd just found out he had to climb onto a Stairmaster and lose fifty pounds by the end of the day and Tony . . .

Her smile slipped.

Tony looked like he wished he'd used that rope on her neck instead of her hands.

"Uh . . . did somebody break a fingernail?" She asked in her best girlish voice. Gotta hand it to her. She wasn't one to let a little tension yank her out of character.

"Cut the act, Ms. Sex in San Francisco," sneered Giovanni.

The truth, on the other hand, could yank the best actor right out of her role. Her smile evaporated.

"The Internet is a wonderful thing. I searched my name to show Tony a recent article on Strands and your site popped up, which reminded me why your name sounded familiar." Giovanni waved a file folder in her direction. "I got this information from the attorney I'd hired to sue you. He told me your real name: Alyssa James."

"Is your alias Erica Allen?" asked Tony. His voice was cold.

Alyssa's heart sank. Just when things seemed to be going so well . . .

"Yes."

"And you wrote the article on me and Chantelle?"

"Yes."

"Be glad she only speculated about you, Tony. She tried to ruin my reputation by writing drivel about me in that gossipy rag of hers and . . ."

For the first time in nearly twenty-four hours, heat that was not related to sex rushed through her veins. She'd giggled and wiggled, pretended to be the Tin Man's twin sister, endured extreme sexual deprivation and torture, and finally had mind-blowing sex with a man who—up until this morning—had shown promise of sticking around and this . . . this . . . sleazy toad had the nerve to call her blog a "gossipy rag"? And then say she wrote drivel? Why—

"For your information, Mr. Maffucci, I report the facts. And, you, sir—"

She jabbed at him with a fingertip as she marched forward. Unfortunately, she forgot about the stilts attached to her ankles and pitched forward.

She put her hands out to catch her fall.

Tony leapt forward to catch her.

Her head smacked his and her world went black.

9

When Alyssa opened her eyes, the first thing she noticed was the jackhammer drilling inside her skull. The second thing was the huge bump that had sprouted from the center of Tony's forehead.

She ran a hand along her forehead and felt a matching bump, though hers felt more like a horn. Which proved that her spill onto the carpet had not been a dream.

"Are you all right?" Tony asked, concern replacing the anger previously etched on his face.

"Yeah," she said. She looked around, noticing that she was lying on the couch where Tony had tortured her with his cock. She tried to sit up.

As Tony reached out to assist her, she noticed his hand. His knuckles were red and his hand had swollen to three times its normal size.

"Did I cause that?" she asked.

"No. He did."

A movement behind him drew her gaze. Giovanni's face was red and puffy and the handkerchief he held under his nose was spotted with blood.

Giovanni walked over to her. "Now that you're awake . . . I'm sorry." Lips pressed together, back straight, he turned on his heel and exited the room.

Alyssa pinched her arm. It hurt, so that meant she wasn't dreaming. Maybe she'd traveled to a parallel world. She closed her eyes and reopened them.

Nope. Tony was still looking at her wearing a warm expression. Wasn't he pissed at her before she fell?

"What's going on?" she asked.

"You fell."

"Yeah, that I remember. But the world seems to have changed a lot since then."

Tony shrugged. "Giovanni called you a sneaky, conniving bitch so I slugged him and told him to apologize."

"And he agreed to apologize, just like that?"

"Uh. He needed a bit more persuading."

She raise a brow.

Tony grinned. "I reasoned with him. I said, 'Giovanni, since you *are* the King of Sleaze and the IRS *did* cite you for income tax evasion, how was Alyssa's article, *IRS Out to Dethrone the King of Sleaze*, detrimental to your reputation?'"

Alyssa snorted. "And when that didn't work?"

Tony's grin widened. "I told him that information about some of his more nefarious dealings would mysteriously appear in your e-mail inbox if he didn't apologize."

Smiling, Alyssa nodded. "Ahhh. That makes more sense. And explains why his apology was so heartfelt."

Tony chuckled.

Alyssa's smile faded.

"Guess I ruined your deal. I'm sorry."

"No, you didn't. I called it off—before I punched him."

Alyssa's mouth dropped open. "You did? Why?"

"I didn't want to do business with a man who talked that way about my date."

You called off a business deal for an emotional reason? For me? Though it warmed her heart, she kept those realizations to herself, saying instead, "But you were mad at me, too. Was it because of the story about Chantelle?"

"No. Despite your humorous, sometimes sarcastic tone, I don't find your blog gossipy."

Alyssa felt her head begin to swell with pride.

"In fact, since I didn't even realize Chantelle had started that rumor about us eloping, I found the article informative. I'm going to have to bookmark your site."

Alyssa smiled. "Thank you."

"You're welcome." He leaned forward and kissed her. As usual, the minute his lips touched hers, major endorphin overload kicked in and all rational thought fled her brain, turning her into one big nerve.

Tony broke the kiss, his eyes looking as glazed as she felt. "Hmmm . . . where was I? Oh yes, why I was mad."

Good thing one of them remembered.

"Because I thought you were playing me, just going out with me to get a story about me hiring a date. But, while you were out, Shannon set me straight."

Alyssa frowned. "You called Shannon to ask her the truth?"

Tony chuckled. "I didn't call Shannon to *ask* her anything. I called her to *accuse* her. I thought she was in on it with you. She explained how you ended up as my date and how you'd promised not to write about me."

"So . . . If I hadn't knocked myself out and I'd told you—instead of Shannon—that I didn't agree to be your date to write about you, would you have believed me?"

"Well, I . . ." He paused and tried again. "I think if you . . ."
And again. "Maybe if . . ."

Alyssa narrowed her eyes. "Shall I take that as a 'no'?"

Tony sighed. "Alyssa, I'll be honest. I don't know."

She pretended like the answer didn't hurt. "Why would you believe Shannon?"

"Because, as she said, what would she have to gain by conspiring with you to write about me? It'd only jeopardize her business."

"Whereas, in my business, I'd have everything to gain." Alyssa laughed humorlessly. "Business is business, right?"

Tony frowned. "You already wrote about me once, Alyssa. Isn't it logical for me to think that you'd try to use this situation to write about me again?"

Leave it to a man to use logic.

"Yeah, I guess so—maybe if you'd found out when we first got here. But, I can't believe you'd think that of me after we . . ." *made love* ". . . had sex."

Tony remained silent.

Alyssa sighed.

How could she feel on the cusp of falling into emotional splendor one second and then feel pushed into an emotional abyss the next? "Well, I guess I won't be calling *The Sin Club* about you," she muttered.

"What? You were going to call into that program and tell the nation I hired a date?"

Alyssa shook her head at Tony's incredulous tone, and stood, shaking off his assistance. "Forget it, Tony. I'm going home."

10

The next day, Alyssa marched into Shannon's office and stalked to her desk.

Shannon looked up and grinned. "I heard—"

"I'm not interested in what you heard. I only agreed to see you in order to collect on my debt." Alyssa paused in front of Shannon and held out her hand.

Shannon frowned. "You'll get payment for the date in thirty days." Her expression changed to one of concern. "Are you experiencing a bit of financial woe?"

"Any woe I'm feeling is all your fault—and it's not financial."

"My fault?"

Alyssa snorted in exasperation and snapped her fingers. "Quit stalling. Pay up."

"Alyssa, I have no idea what you're talking about."

"You said you'd pay me if I propositioned someone. Well, I propositioned Tony and I want my money."

Shannon took Alyssa's hand and put it in the air, high-fiving her. "Way to go! When did you do it? Wait a minute, aren't you mad at Tony?"

"Yes, I am mad at Tony but I did it before then."

"Well, when are you going to do *it*?"

Alyssa stepped back and sank into the lime green chair. Instantly deflated, she sighed—loudly—in defeat. "I already did *it*. Yesterday."

"You broke the contract?"

"Don't screech, Shannon. It's unprofessional."

"Alyssa, I could get my business license revoked. The state—"

Alyssa waved a hand. "Yes, yes, I know. Your words rang in my ears day and night. I had to give in just to get them to stop."

"Oh, no, this is not my fault. You promised."

"Did you really think I could stick to that? Could you? I tried!"

Shannon stared into space, her eyes glazed with worry. "This is bad."

"Don't worry. Tony promised not to tell anyone."

Shannon's gaze snapped to hers. Her lips twisted. "They all promise that."

"What? You mean this happens often?"

Shannon leaned back in her chair and closed her eyes. "Yes. Why do you think I have the contract? Why do you think I stress it over and over again?"

Alyssa's mouth dropped open. "I can't believe you made me feel so guilty, like I'd be betraying our friendship, risking your livelihood—"

"You have risked my livelihood. He still might report me to the state, since you're mad at him! Alyssa, can't you make nice—"

Exasperation instantly reappeared. "Oh, for heaven's sake,

he's not—" She paused and narrowed her eyes. "Wait a minute, how did you know that I'm mad at him?"

At that moment, Shannon's phone buzzed. She answered it. "Please send him in, Charlotte." Shannon rose to her feet.

An awful dose of déjà vu prickled Alyssa. "Shannon—"

Shannon beamed, looking at a spot past Alyssa's left ear. "Tony, what a pleasant surprise."

Oh, so now it's Tony? Alyssa glared at Shannon before turning around.

Her glare dissolved. Oxygen was sucked from her lungs. Anger evaporated from her mind and lust blossomed in her groin.

Tony sauntered into the room, his long legs encased in stonewashed jeans, his buff chest decorated with a snug fitting T-shirt. His satiny hair was loose and tucked behind one ear. His eyes glimmered, his smile dazzled.

He looked boyish and playful and delicious.

"Thanks for your help, Shannon."

"No problem. Well, I'm sure you two have a lot to discuss." She walked from behind the desk and headed toward the door.

Alyssa attempted to summon her anger. "No, we don't." She muttered.

They both ignored her. Shannon closed the door softly behind her. Tony stopped in front of her.

"I have something for you." He said, removing his iPod and portable headphones from his pocket.

"Oh, you shouldn't have," she squealed, doing her best Lissy impersonation. "Diamonds disguised as an iPod."

"Alyssa, please listen." He held them out to her.

With a long-suffering sigh, Alyssa slipped the ear pieces into her ears.

Tony pressed play.

Dr. Love filled her head. ". . . so we're going to do things a bit differently with our next caller. I'm going to let him sin on the air. Tony, you're on."

"Thanks, Tom—er, Dr. Love," said Tony.

Alyssa looked at Tony. "You?" she breathed.

"Me," said the real-life Tony.

Alyssa turned her attention back to the recorded Tony.

"I'm a private person so this is a bit rough . . ." His voice had a quaver Alyssa had never heard.

"Take your time, Tony."

"Well . . . my life was ruled by business decisions but then I met Alyssa and, well, she taught me that sometimes you need to make emotional decisions. Like, not to purchase a profitable business from a person you despise, who insults someone you . . . care about and, well, most importantly to believe in someone because your gut—not your mind—tells you they're telling the truth. So. That's my sin—allowing emotion—in the form of Alyssa—into my life. And I hope she'll take me . . ."

A lump grew in Alyssa's throat. Tony, the mystery man who kept his personal life private, had admitted to all that on the air. For her. To convince her.

Alyssa whipped the earphones out of her ears. She threw herself into Tony's arms and hugged him and kissed him and punched him.

"I'll take you," she said softly, smiling up at him.

"Good," said Tony. "Seal it with a kiss."

And she did.

Epilogue

Tommy "Dr. Love" Jones turned off the mike and took off his headphones. Placing his hands at his temples, he massaged his head with circular strokes.

The nights were starting to feel longer.

The calls were starting to drain, rather than excite.

His mind was starting to feel tired, rather than energized.

What was wrong with him? His hard work had netted him the number one talk show in the nation, he was talking his way to wealth beyond his imagination and yet . . .

Over the last few weeks, something was missing. Something felt off.

A tap on the glass brought his head up. Judy, his assistant who manned the phones, eyed him with concern.

You okay? she mouthed.

He forced a smile and nodded.

She smiled, gave him a thumbs-up, and exited the booth.

The studio was quiet. Tommy was alone. At work, as he was in his personal life.

Tommy sighed and looked down at his notepad. He reread

the notes he'd jotted during the commercial breaks—ideas for a new direction for *The Sin Club*.

They were good. The director would love them.

Maybe that's all he needed. A change. A new challenge.

Yeah, that was probably it.

Shaking off his melancholy, he rose, suddenly in a hurry to leave. Sadie would be waiting, tail wagging, tongue lolling, anxious to welcome him home.

Author's Note

While Sharice and her escapades in *The Sin Club* are fictional, the Dirty Minnie is not. This drink was created specifically for me by a delightful bartender at Triple Play—a bar located in the Underground in Atlanta, Georgia, while I was doing "research." Here's the recipe:

Dirty Minnie

1½ ounces of Stoli Strasberi
Splash of Stoli Vodka
¾ ounces of Amaretto
Splash of Grenadine
Splash of Sprite
Splash of Sweet and Sour
Garnish with lemon and cherry

It's delicious, but deadly, so drink it with caution. For the story behind the drink, as well as more information about my books and blog, please visit me at www.RachelleChase.com.

Sasha White has made a date
with a SEXY DEVIL!

On sale now!

Prologue

She couldn't look away.

He had her wrists above her head, pinned against the mattress, and his eyes locked on hers as his hips thrust forward to slide gently into her body. Her pulse raced and she wrapped her legs around his waist, holding him tight. His rhythm picked up speed and she whimpered; her sex tightening around him, her body trembling with the strength of her approaching orgasm. Her heavy eyelids drooped, but she couldn't let them fall, couldn't look away from the well of emotions overflowing from his eyes.

"I love you, Gina," he whispered.

Joy filled her and she cried out, every fiber within her strung taut as she squeezed him between her thighs. She squeezed harder and thrust her hips again—and felt nothing but emptiness. He was gone. Her thighs pressed only against each other.

A growl of frustration echoed through Gina Devlin's empty bedroom as she opened her eyes and pressed a hand against her heated forehead.

Another dream. Another faceless lover with eyes that looked deep into her soul and filled her heart while he filled her body.

Flopping over onto her back in the queen-size bed, Gina kicked at the tangled sheets and let the cool air dance across her overheated skin.

She was used to dreams waking her up. When she was a little girl, all her premonitions had come in the form of dreams. But as she grew, so had her skill at manipulating and controlling her gift. Now she could use touch, smell, and sometimes, strength of will, to bring forth a vision if she needed to.

And normally she could block them with equal ease.

She'd had to learn how to block the random psychic vibrations that floated around people or she wouldn't have been able to live a normal life. But at night, when she sought peace in sleep, sometimes the dreams still came.

The dream with the faceless lover declaring his love had been with her for years, and she wondered if it really was a premonition or just wishful thinking on her part.

She'd longed for a man to love her as she was for so long, it was more fantasy than dream.

Closing her eyes once more, Gina Devlin trailed a hand over her belly and past the small patch of tight curls. Trying to forget the familiar ache of loneliness in her heart, she concentrated on easing the ache of emptiness between her thighs.

1

Caleb Mann strode through the heavy glass doors of Fusion Cafe and continued straight to the service counter without looking left or right. The air-conditioning inside the café was a welcome relief from the humid heat of mid May in Pearson, British Columbia. It also took the edge off his nerves.

Mug of strong, black coffee firmly in hand, Caleb stepped to the side of the counter, and scanned the room carefully.

The sunlight bounced off the surface of Pearson Lake, directly across the street, brightening the small café. Colorful paintings on the walls and mismatched furniture gave it a funky, comfortable feel that was reflected in the diverse clientele. A slick-looking businessman stood a couple of feet away, impatiently ordering a fluffy latte from the frowning counter girl. An older lady and a girl who was probably her granddaughter sat with a coloring book in front of them.

None were who he was looking for.

He disregarded the twentysomething male engrossed in a novel nearby and briefly considered the woman by the window. Well dressed, with long dark hair, she sat ramrod straight as she watched people come and go. She was pretty, but Caleb didn't think she was the type of woman his brother would be friends with. Uncertain, he let his gaze slide away.

Then he saw *her*.

Removing his sunglasses, he gave the woman a slow perusal. She'd isolated herself by sitting at a small corner table, head bent over a notepad of some kind. Yet she still seemed approachable. The invisible wall that emanated from most people when they wanted to be left alone wasn't there.

She was dressed casually in a short camouflage skirt and a tight black tank top that made it impossible to ignore her pert breasts. If for some unknown reason he hadn't noticed her mouthwatering cleavage, he'd certainly have given the length of tanned flesh exposed by the short skirt a second glance. It had to be her.

Caleb had expected nothing less from his little brother than to set him up with a real looker. What he hadn't expected was his own primal reaction to her—the way his blood heated and his stomach clenched when he looked at her—or the way her inky black hair, which was full of vivid red streaks and skimmed across her pale shoulders, made his fingers itch with the urge to touch . . . to brush it aside so he could nibble on her tender flesh.

His reaction surprised him, but for once he didn't try to contain or control it. After all, if she was a friend of his "work hard–play harder" younger brother, chances were she was also a party girl—a bad girl.

Oh, yeah, he thought to himself. The total opposite of what he normally looked for in the fairer sex, and exactly what he *needed*.

Detail-oriented guy that he was, Caleb leaned against the counter and studied her for a minute. Skimpy clothes flaunted bare limbs, bright purple polish sparkled on her fingertips, and silver jewelry flashed when she shifted in the filtered sunlight. There was also a tattoo on the inside of her wrist—very . . . exciting. He willed her to lift her head so he could see her face clearly, only to have his breath catch in his throat when she did so.

Flawless skin smoothed over high cheekbones, tiny white teeth nibbled at a full pink lip, dark eyebrows flared over almond-shaped eyes. He couldn't see their color from where he was, but it didn't matter. Her classic beauty and outrageous sex appeal called to him unlike anything, or anyone, ever had.

He wanted her, instantly and unequivocally.

Shrugging his suddenly tense shoulders, Caleb pushed off from the counter. *You're not here to find your soul mate*, he reminded himself, *just someone to let loose with*.

He was tired of everyone ragging on him for being a workaholic. Hell, if he hadn't worked so hard for the past ten years, Gabe wouldn't have been able to go to college. Someone had had to pay the bills after their parents died. Plus, his work was satisfying in a way his player of a brother would never understand, so the nagging hadn't really bothered him.

Until his last girlfriend dumped him because he was too "old and settled" for her, that is. *Then* he'd felt a bit of a sting. He was only thirty-three, for God's sake!

Even then her comments hadn't really hurt him. Not until she'd turned the sting into a downright festering burn by adding that his good looks couldn't compensate for his lack of imagination in the romance department, let alone the bedroom.

Anger, and a twist of uncertainty, burned a hole in his gut. That had been hitting below the belt, literally.

Lack of imagination? He had plenty of imagination. And the wild-child woman his little brother had set him up with was going to help him prove it.

Halting next to her table, he pasted a winning smile on his face and opened his mouth.

"Excuse me. Christina?"

When Gina Devlin realized the question was directed at her, she huffed out a grateful breath and tossed aside her charcoal pencil. Normally she didn't welcome interruptions when she was working, but her temperamental muse had deserted her, taking any semblance of artistic talent along with him. That made it pretty damn hard to get the sketches for her new commission down.

Eager for a distraction, Gina leaned back in the spindly chair and looked over the wall of muscle standing next to her corner table with a big grin on his gorgeous face. And her skin immediately began to itch from the inside out.

He was her favorite type of distraction—big and male.

The buttoned-up shirt and pressed jeans he wore did nothing to detract from the wide shoulders and slim hips they covered. But, in her mind, they did label him a stickler for the rules, and that made him totally not her type. Only a real stick-in-the-mud irons his *jeans*.

Not being her type didn't stop her eyes from continuing to skim appreciatively over his trim hips—and the impressive package between them, too. And of course she couldn't stop there, so she mentally drooled over his muscled thighs for a long moment before raising her gaze to meet his.

A steady gaze that was vaguely familiar.

Shaking off that thought, she realized he'd called her Christina. The little devil inside her strained at the leash she'd kept him on for the last six months. Poking her with his pointy tail, he screamed, "Do it! Do it!"

Before she could think twice, her lips parted, and the words tumbled out. "I prefer Tina." *It's closer to Gina.*